Halloween Energy Vampire

Blasters

DAVID LLOYD STRAUSS

*Dedicated to those brave souls navigating
their darkness, looking for their light.*

In Shadows Deep, the Energy Vampires Dwell
By David Lloyd Strauss

In shadows deep, the vampires dwell,
With whispers dark, they cast their spell,
They creep and crawl, unseen by day,
But in the night, they find their prey.

With fangs of doubt, they sink within,
Turning light to shadowed sin,
They feed on fears, on hopes undone,
Leaving hearts cold, far from the sun.

Yet in the dark, a spark ignites,
A soul prepared for haunted fights,
With courage strong and laughter near,
You face the night, dispel the fear.

Through winding paths of eerie gloom,
You have walked through every haunted room,
The vampires shriek, they try to stay,
But giggles bright chase them away.

For in your heart, a light does glow,
A flame that energy vampires know,
Can't be dimmed, nor snuffed, nor swayed,
It's your power—forever displayed.

So journey on, with giggles bright,
Through every shadowed, haunted night,
For in your hands, the power lies,
To banish fears and claim the prize.

In shadows deep, they once did dwell,
But you have broken their cursed spell,
With heart and soul, and giggles too,
You have turned the darkness into something new.

Contents

Unmasking your Inner Energy Vampire

Energy Vampires Amongst Us

With deep gratitude for my mentors.

Sharon Lechter

Mike Lechter

Angela Totman

Welcome letter from David Strauss

Dear Seeker of Light,

As you embark on the journey through the pages of *Halloween Energy Vampire Blasters*, I want to share with you a belief that has been forged through the trials of my own life—a belief that the most important decision we will ever make is choosing the people we associate with, those who stand closest to us in our daily lives.

My life has been a long and testing journey. I was a runaway at 15 after the death of my mother, thrown into a world where I had to find my own way. I put myself through high school and college, determined to carve out a path despite the odds. Then, there was the moment when I was exploring ancient Anasazi ruins in Chaco Canyon, New Mexico, and a rock fell from above, and struck me on the head—a literal hit that became the reset I didn't know I needed. It was a wake-up call, a turning point that made me reevaluate every nook and cranny of my life, resolve emotional pain from my childhood—everything, including the people I allowed into my life.

It was through these experiences that I learned the profound importance of the company we keep. The people around us shape our world, influencing our happiness, health, and overall quality of life. This book is my way of passing on the lessons I've learned, to help you sharpen your awareness and see the shadows for what they truly are. When you can identify the negative influences—the Energy Vampires lurking in the corners of your life—you gain the power to elevate your associations.

With this awareness, you can choose to surround yourself with those who uplift you, who bring light into your world, and who help you shine even brighter. My hope is that this journey empowers you to make those choices wisely, to protect your energy, and to reclaim your light.

May you find the strength to surround yourself with those who add to your joy and leave the shadows behind.

With courage and light,

David Strauss

Welcome, brave soul, to "Halloween Energy Vampire Blasters."

The ultimate spell book for reclaiming your precious energy and banishing those wicked forces that drain your mojo.

In these haunted pages, you'll find the tools, the spells, and the ancient wisdom to arm yourself against the dark entities that lurk in the shadows of your life.

Here, you shall uncover the secrets to identifying, confronting, and ultimately overcoming the sinister Energy Vampires that seek to sap your strength and steal your joy.

Prepare your spirit, sharpen your wits, and light your lanterns bright—for tonight, you embark on a journey through the eerie lairs of these vampiric fiends.

With each page you turn, you'll draw closer to the dawn, where you, fully empowered, will stand victorious over the forces that once sought to drag you down.

So, ready your stake, steady your nerves, and let's dive deep into the night. Your ultimate arsenal against the Energy Vampires awaits, and with it, the power to reclaim the light that is rightfully yours.

Welcome to your journey.

You're in for one spellbinding adventure!

PART I

Unmasking the Energy Vampires

In the opening act of this spooky saga, you'll learn to spot the Energy Vampires lurking in the hidden corners of your life. These fiendish foes feed on your light, leaving you drained and weary. But fear not! As an apprentice Energy Vampire Blaster, you'll soon discover the power within you to banish these creatures and reclaim your energy, turning the tables on those who would dim your glow.

Introduction

Here Begins the Journey to Become a Halloween Energy Vampire Blaster

Greetings, fearless seeker of the light! You are about to set foot on a road of discovery like no other—one that will awaken your hidden powers and transform you into a mighty Halloween Energy Vampire Blaster. But beware, this journey of discovery is not for the faint of heart. Along the way, you will encounter the most dreaded creatures of all—Energy Vampires.

What does it mean to become a Halloween Energy Vampire Blaster? It means becoming a daring warrior of light, armed with mystical tools and ancient wisdom to fend off those who seek to drain your energy and dim your inner glow. This is no ordinary title; it is a badge of honor earned through courage, resilience, and a touch of magical mischief.

As you travel this road of discovery, you will master the following:

Guardian of Your Glow: Protect your energy from those who try to siphon it away, setting firm boundaries that keep your spirit shining bright amidst the dark.

Warrior of Light: With a flick of your wand (or a well-placed boundary), you'll blast away negativity, transforming dark forces into harmless shadows that dare not linger in your presence.

Master of Resilience: Build an impenetrable fortress of self-care, ensuring that no Energy Vampire can breach your defenses or dim your sparkle. Your inner strength will become your greatest ally.

Champion for Others: As you rise to the rank of Halloween Energy Vampire Blaster, you'll not only protect yourself but also inspire and guide others to reclaim their energy and fend off the forces of darkness.

This road of discovery will empower you to wield your newfound abilities with flair and confidence, turning your life into a beacon of light and joy—no matter what monsters may lurk in the shadows. With each step you take, you'll come closer to mastering the art of energy protection and embracing your role as a Halloween Energy Vampire Blaster. So, gather your courage, ignite your inner fire, and prepare to walk this extraordinary path.

The night is full of mysteries, and the road ahead is fraught with challenges. But with each discovery, you'll grow stronger, more resilient, and more attuned to the magical forces within and around you. Welcome to the road of discovery—your transformation begins now!

The 13 Sinister Energy Vampires

As you prepare to take your first steps on this road of discovery, beware of the 13 Energy Vampires that lurk in the shadows, waiting to drain your spirit before you even realize it.

Each of these 13 vampires has its sinister method of stealing your strength. Some thrive on constant drama, pulling you into their never-ending web of chaos. Others drain you through relentless complaints, wearing you down with their negativity until you're left with nothing but exhaustion. And then there's the most devious vampire of them all—the one inside your head, whispering doubts and fears, eroding your confidence with every passing thought.

These are no ordinary foes. They may not wear capes or sleep in coffins, but they're every bit as deadly, hiding behind familiar faces and everyday situations, quietly sapping your strength while you remain blissfully unaware. But fear not, for knowledge is your first line of defense. As you embark on this eerie journey, you'll begin to see the Energy Vampires for what they truly are—silent predators feeding on your peace of mind.

Are you ready to uncover the emotional suckers that have been lurking in the shadows of your life? Brace yourself as we dive into the many Lairs of the 13 Energy Vampires.

Bats Eye View...

And now for a bat's-eye view of these 13 Energy Vampires before we swoop down for a closer look at each lurking fiend.

Beware the Soul Suckers

In your daily life, you may have encountered the Soul Suckers—those shadowy figures known as takers and narcissists. These sinister beings don't just crave attention; they feed on the very essence of your being, leaving you drained and hollow. Often hiding in plain sight, they are all about what they can get, not what they can give. Selfish and self-absorbed, yet seductive and charming, they have strong personalities and a deep need for significance and control. They twist their perspective to always be right and will lure you in with their charm, making you feel "needed" only to further their own sense of love, significance, and power.

Phantoms of Chaos

These are the black hole of attention cravers. They seek validation and approval at all costs. Their life is an endless soap opera of whining, disappointments, false hopes, complaints, and gossip. They believe that the easiest way to get love and attention is by broadcasting their problems to everyone until someone consoles them, gives them attention, and makes them feel validated and loved.

Denial Demons

These are the Debbie Downers. They live a life of perpetual blame and of being a victim—never accepting responsibility for the challenges in their life. They look for reasons outside of themselves to justify their failures and shortcomings. They live this way because they have deep fears of rejection and failure. Through an unhealthy form of self-preservation, they deflect their problems and postpone the pain of growing and maturing.

Wailing Spirits

These Vampires do not believe that they deserve or can have what they want, and so they have developed a habit of feeling mentally and emotionally deprived. Rarely do they feel genuine happiness for other people's achievements, nor their own. They live in a continuous emotional loop of jealousy, envy, and fear of missing out. They are addicted to feeling insignificant and unworthy, so they live a life of quiet desperation. They do this because they cannot handle the uncertainty of life, and so they play small and pretend they are helpless.

Cauldron Crawlers

Crabs are desperately insecure individuals who claw others down in order to build themselves up. Known as the kings and queens of insecurity, they are experts at sowing discord and dragging others into their misery, often pitting people against each other or stirring up conflict just to be at the center of the turmoil. They thrive in environments of chaos and confusion, where they can manipulate situations to their advantage. By keeping others off balance, Crabs mask their own insecurities and maintain a semblance of control. Quick to criticize and undermine others' achievements, they fear that someone else's success might highlight their own inadequacies, so they habitually create problems and escalate minor issues to keep the focus away from their shortcomings.

Gloom Mongers

The master of playing the perpetual victim, they are always stuck in a cycle of misfortune and sorrow. They thrive on turning every minor inconvenience into a major catastrophe, seeking endless sympathy and support from those around them. This constant complainer brings a cloud of pessimism wherever they go, never seeing the silver lining and always expecting the worst. To add to the emotional drain, they frequently employ guilt trips, making others feel responsible for their perpetual unhappiness. Their need for validation and assistance creates a lopsided relationship where the Gloom Monger relies heavily on others to lift them out of their self-imposed despair. They drain the energy and spirit of those involved, pulling everyone into their web of woe and expecting others to take on the emotional burden of their never-ending grievances. Their life is an ongoing saga of complaints, guilt trips, and pessimism, with no resolution in sight.

Shadow Controller

This Energy Vampire thrives on intimidation and control. They use fear, aggression, and manipulation to dominate others, often targeting those they perceive as weaker. The Bully feeds off the power they feel when they belittle, threaten, or push others around. Their interactions are marked by a lack of empathy and an insatiable need to assert their superiority. They might disguise their behavior as "tough love" or claim they're just being "honest," but their true motive is to maintain control and keep others off balance. The Bully drains energy by creating a constant atmosphere of tension and anxiety, leaving their victims feeling powerless and insecure. Over time, their relentless aggression can erode self-esteem, making it difficult for others to stand up for themselves or break free from the toxic dynamic.

Chronic Critics

The Critic finds fault in everything and everyone around them. Nothing is ever good enough, and they are quick to point out flaws, mistakes, and shortcomings. The Critic's weapon is their sharp tongue, using constant criticism to undermine confidence and spread negativity. They believe their harsh judgments are justified, often disguising their relentless negativity as "constructive feedback" or "just trying to help." However, their real aim is to assert their own superiority by diminishing the efforts and achievements of others. The Critic drains energy by creating an environment of doubt and discouragement, where people feel they can never meet expectations or do anything right. This relentless critique can sap the joy out of accomplishments and make it difficult for others to feel proud of their work or confident in their abilities.

Deceptive Gaslighters

The Gaslighter thrives on manipulation, subtly twisting facts and situations to make others doubt their own perceptions and memories. They constantly shift blame and create confusion, making those around them question their reality. This form of psychological manipulation erodes self-confidence and creates a sense of dependency on the Gaslighter. Their tactics are exhausting and emotionally draining, as they undermine the mental stability and self-assurance of their targets.

Toxic Gossips

The Gossip spreads rumors and shares secrets, reveling in the drama they create. They thrive on the chaos and conflict that their words stir up, and they pull others into their web by encouraging them to participate in the gossip. This behavior not only drains energy but also destroys trust and fosters a toxic environment. The Gossip's relentless pursuit of attention through negative means leaves those around them feeling uneasy and constantly on guard.

Needy Ones

The needy ones constantly seek attention, validation, and reassurance. They rely heavily on others for emotional support, often demanding more than what's reasonable. This neediness can drain the energy of those who are always expected to provide comfort and guidance. The needy one struggles with self-sufficiency, and their constant demands can become overwhelming, leaving others feeling depleted and burdened by their emotional needs.

Love Lane Vampires

When the person you share your life with becomes the primary source of your emotional exhaustion, it's important to recognize if they might be an Energy Vampire. If they consistently focus on the negative, dragging you into a similar mindset, this could be a sign. Emotional manipulation is another red flag—using guilt, blame, or emotional blackmail to control you, which can leave you feeling powerless. A lack of support is also common, where instead of uplifting you, they dismiss your dreams and make you doubt yourself. If your partner demands constant attention, leaving little room for your own needs, or frequently criticizes and blames you, chipping away at your self-esteem, they are likely an Energy Vampire. If you find yourself in this situation, take massive action to carefully and responsibly get help.

The 13 Energy Vampires

Let's have some fun and shine a lantern on each of these shadowy figures that lurk in the corners of your life—those sneaky Energy Vampires that drain your vitality and keep you from living your best life. Each of these vampires has a unique way of sinking its fangs into your energy, leaving you feeling drained, overwhelmed, and stuck in a cycle of negativity. So, gather your courage, and let's take a closer look at these sinister characters. As we delve into their tricks and traps, you'll learn how to banish them from your life once and for all. Ready to face the darkness? Let's begin!

THE 1ˢᵀ LAIR

Soul Suckers

The Self-Absorbed Takers

Beware of the sinister yet charming Soul Suckers—the narcissists lurking in the shadows of your social circle. These emotional parasites are the Draculas of your daily life, always ready to sink their fangs into your energy, draining you dry with every encounter. These fiends don't wait for the cover of night—oh no, they thrive in broad daylight, basking in the admiration they so desperately crave. They are all about themselves, and they'll drain the life out of you to keep their egos well-fed.

Every interaction with a Soul Sucker feels like stepping into a well-laid trap. You're caught in their web, where everything suddenly revolves around their desires. Planning a group outing? Forget it—it's now about their favorite spot, their stories, their endless tales of glory. If you ever find yourself in a conversation that feels like it's spiraling into a black hole, you're likely in the clutches of a Soul Sucker.

These Energy Vampires aren't just attention seekers—they're master manipulators. They twist conversations to keep themselves at the center, overshadow your victories with their own exaggerated achievements, and constantly seek validation, all while offering nothing in return. They're emotional manipulators who play with your feelings, making you feel guilty for not catering to their every whim, and if you dare establish boundaries, they'll cast you as the villain for not being at their constant beck and call.

But the true terror of these vampires lies in their mastery of emotional trickery. In the dark corridors of relationships, Soul Suckers weave spells of gaslighting, love-bombing, and passive-aggressive jabs that leave you defenseless. One moment, they're the perfect picture of adoration, making you feel like the center of their universe. The next, they're dragging you down into a pit of doubt and despair, warping your reality with every twisted word. It's like being trapped in a cursed carnival—glittering lights above, but beneath, it's all smoke and mirrors, designed to drain the very essence of your being.

Victims of these narcissistic ghouls often find themselves caught in a nightmarish loop of confusion and self-doubt; their confidence slowly bled dry by the constant emotional torment. The wounds they leave aren't visible, but they run deep—scars that linger long after the Soul Sucker has moved on to their next victim.

The Allure of the Givers

In the shadowy world of Soul Suckers, there's nothing more enticing than the warm glow of a Giver's heart. These generous, warm-hearted souls shine like beacons in the night, attracting Soul Suckers with an irresistible pull. Givers, by their very nature, radiate care and compassion, often placing others' needs above their own. This selfless light is what draws Soul Suckers in, creating a lopsided relationship where the Giver is slowly drained of their energy and vigor, like a candle flickering out in a wind-chilled room.

Soul Suckers are masterful at exploiting the kindness and empathy of Givers, weaving a web of manipulation that traps them in a cycle of giving while receiving nothing in return. Givers, who prefer to avoid conflict and seek harmony, can find themselves ensnared in the Soul Sucker's sorcery, manipulated into believing that they are responsible for the Soul Sucker's happiness or emotional stability. The result? The Giver becomes a victim of the Soul Sucker's dark magic, slowly losing their sense of self in the process, their light dimming under the weight of endless demands.

Understanding the Soul Sucker's Game

At their creepy core, Soul Suckers view relationships as dark transactions—what can this person offer me? Their insatiable thirst for the spotlight often eclipses any real capacity for genuine, selfless love. Here's a glimpse into their sinister playbook:

The Conversational Hoarder: Ever felt like a mere whisper in your own story? That's a Soul Sucker for you, dominating discussions like a greedy phantom at a midnight feast. They steer the conversation back to themselves, leaving you as nothing more than a shadow in the eerie tale of your own life.

The Chronic One-Upper: Share a victory, and they'll overshadow it with something grander, casting your achievements into the cold shadows of their towering tales. It's their sinister method of keeping the upper hand, leaving you questioning your worth as they bask in their own ghostly glow.

The Validation Seeker: Don't be fooled by their attentive act—it's an illusion. These Soul Suckers are on an eternal quest for compliments and affirmations, like restless spirits craving acknowledgment from the living. They drain your energy, offering little in return, their echoing demands for validation haunting your every step.

The Emotional Manipulator: Beware the puppeteers of guilt, Soul Suckers who twist reality with a wicked grin. They'll make you feel guilty for not catering to their every whim, pulling your strings with eerie precision. If things don't go their way, the blame falls squarely on you, as they weave their dark magic to keep you in their thrall.

The Boundary Pusher: Personal space? A concept lost on these relentless spirits. They demand your time and energy like unyielding phantoms, showing no regard for reciprocation. Dare to set boundaries, and they'll cast you as the villain in their obsessed narrative, always at the ready to pull you back into their grasp.

The Gaslighter: Soul Suckers often employ the dark art of gaslighting, turning your reality into a foggy maze of confusion. They deny the truth, distort your memories, and twist your perceptions until you're left questioning your own sanity. They are the masters of illusion, leaving you lost in their labyrinth of lies.

The Sympathy Seeker: Masters of the tragic tale, these vampires play the victim to perfection, weaving sob stories that pull at your heartstrings until you're ensnared in their web. They exploit your empathy, drawing you deeper into their twisted narrative, where your role is to serve their endless need for attention and sympathy.

The Commitment Phoebe: In the murky waters of relationships, these shadowy figures avoid commitment, slipping through your grasp just when you think you have got them figured out. They keep you off-balance, preventing deep emotional connections as they maintain control from the shadows, never fully revealing themselves.

Conflict Avoidance: A Soul Sucker's Playground

For Soul Suckers, someone who shies away from confrontation is a treasure trove. They relish a smooth, unchallenged existence. A partner who avoids conflict is less likely to confront them or stand up against them, allowing the Soul Sucker to dominate without resistance. It's like possessing a remote control for the relationship—press a button, and the conflict-avoider responds, often bending over backward to maintain peace.

Kindness: A Double-Edged Sword

There's something irresistibly attractive to a Soul Sucker about someone compassionate and willing to help, to understand, to support. Soul Suckers know precisely how to exploit this kindness for their own ends. They might play the role of the victim or the misunderstood hero, manipulating your compassion as a tool for their own benefit.

Lovers and Romantics: Prime Targets

Those who pour their hearts into relationships are ideal targets for Soul Suckers. These charmers can conjure a whirlwind romance that feels like a dream come true. But beware—it's often just an illusion. The Soul Sucker plays the role of the perfect partner only to abandon the facade once they have you ensnared.

Liberating Yourself from the Soul Suckers

Now that you have entered the lair of the Soul Suckers, it's time to recognize these sinister figures for what they are. See through their tricks, reclaim your power, and banish them from your life. The only way to protect your energy is to break free from their web of manipulation and take back control of your narrative.

Liberating yourself from these toxic entanglements can feel like untangling a web spun by a master manipulator. But with a little self-awareness and support, you can drive a stake through their hold on your life and banish them from your world for good.

Phantoms of Chaos

The Sinister Drama Queens

As the witching hour approaches, it's time to sweep away the cobwebs of toxic entanglements and confront the Phantoms of Chaos—the Drama Queens who weave their sinister webs of emotional chaos. These Energy Vampires are like malevolent puppet masters, orchestrating every situation to ensure they're the star of the show. Drama Queens thrive on attention, using it as their lifeblood, and they'll go to any length to make sure all eyes are on them.

They delight in transforming minor inconveniences into cataclysmic events, ensnaring everyone around them in a whirlwind of their own making. Their lives are a never-ending parade of crises, each more urgent and dramatic than the last, leaving no room for anyone else's needs or emotions. These masters of manipulation are experts at twisting reality to fit their dark narrative, drawing you into their theatrical world where you're expected to play the supporting role in their eerie drama.

When you're seeking to banish these shadowy ties from your life, beware—the Drama Queens are the plot twist lurking just around the corner, ready to ensnare you once more. Let's unravel their webs and expose the ghouls beneath, before they draw you deeper into their chilling tales.

The Allure of the Phantoms of Chaos

The Drama Queens have an eerie, magnetic pull. Their lives play out like a never-ending horror flick, filled with chilling twists and bone-chilling turns that draw you in. The intensity of their emotions is like a potion brewed in the darkest cauldron, intoxicating and irresistible. But beware—while it's thrilling to watch from a distance, getting caught up in their nightmare is a whole different terror.

Caught in the Web

Falling into the web of these Phantoms feels like being ensnared by a cunning spider lurking in the shadows. At first, it's exhilarating—you're the hero in their dark and twisted saga, the one destined to save the day. But soon, the thrill fades, and you find yourself tangled in their sticky threads. The more you struggle, the tighter their web becomes, draining your energy and leaving no room for your own desires and dreams.

The Emotional Rollercoaster

Living with a Phantom of Chaos is like riding a haunted rollercoaster, one that only spirals up and down through the darkest of nights, never offering a moment of peace. One minute, you're their savior, the light in their shadowy world. The next, you're cast as the villain in their macabre melodrama, blamed for every sinister twist of fate. This emotional whiplash leaves you spinning, lost in a dizzying labyrinth of fear and confusion.

The Quest for Stability

After being trapped in their web, you begin to yearn for something more solid, more real. You crave friendships and relationships built on mutual respect and trust, not this endless parade of ghostly turmoil. You realize that true connection doesn't need theatrics to be deep and meaningful—it's about consistency, trust, and a bond that doesn't need the shadows to thrive. These are the qualities often eclipsed by the Drama Queen's endless show.

Stepping Away

Breaking free from the grasp of these Phantoms is no easy task, but is a necessary exorcism for your soul. It's about recognizing that you deserve peace and that your spirit needs to dwell in a sanctuary free from constant hauntings. This doesn't mean you don't care—it means you're finally prioritizing your mental and emotional health. It's a step toward finding friendships and relationships that elevate your spirit, rather than dragging it into the dark abyss of perpetual drama.

Craving Calm Waters

As the shadows fade and the thrill of drama loses its grip on your heart, you begin to crave the calm, serene waters of stability. You seek friendships and relationships where disagreements don't morph into monstrous melodramas, where peace isn't just the eerie calm before another storm, but genuine serenity. You start to understand that authentic connections thrive on mutual respect, understanding, and those quiet moments of intimacy that aren't riddled by endless conflicts.

Spotting a Phantom of Chaos

Picture this: a friend, family member, or coworker who can turn a spilled potion into a three-act tragedy, complete with eerie sound effects and ghostly wails. They've got a flair for the dramatic, transforming the smallest of problems into towering, haunted houses filled with phantoms of their own creation. Whether at home, in the office, or among friends, they're always the lead in every dark tale, with a script overflowing with woes, tragedies, and crises. It's like living with a reality TV star from the underworld—except there's no off button, and the scares are all too real. If you find yourself constantly ensnared in their latest catastrophe or tiptoeing through their minefield of emotions, you have got a Drama Queen on your hands, ready to pull you into their endless night of theatrics.

The Victim Player

Ah, the Victim Player—a master of the horrific art of self-pity! These shadowy figures are always the tragic hero in their own dreadful tales, forever casting themselves as the downtrodden soul in a world of wicked foes. Every conversation with them is like reading a new chapter in a gothic novel of endless woes, each more embellished than the last to ensnare your sympathy and keep you dancing to their mournful tune.

The Crisis Creator

Enter the Crisis Creator, a being who thrives in the eerie glow of chaos and calamity. In their world, peace is but a distant memory, replaced by a never-ending parade of crises. Like a wolf drawn to the thrill of the hunt, they conjure disasters from the simplest of spats, expecting you to don your hero's cape time and time again. Beware, for their drama is a curse that will leave you drained and weary.

The Gossip Monger

Beware the Gossip Monger, a cunning creature who feeds on the whispers of the night. This person relishes in the dark art of spreading tales, weaving webs of deceit to entangle you in their sinister plots. They thrive in the shadows, adding fuel to the fires of discord, all to ensure they remain the puppeteer behind the scenes. In their presence, the air is thick with secrets, and every word they speak drips with the venom of manipulation.

The Overreactor

Ah, the Overreactor, a tempestuous spirit who turns the smallest slight into a cataclysmic storm. In their twisted reality, every spilled potion or misplaced broomstick becomes a full-blown catastrophe, sucking you into their whirlwind of overblown emotions. Their screams echo through their dark halls, leaving you wondering if you'll ever find peace in the eye of their never-ending storm.

The Emotional Extortionist

And now, meet the Emotional Extortionist who wields their feelings like a cursed dagger. With tears that flow like rivers and tantrums that shake the very foundations of your sanity, they ensnare you in their emotional traps. They demand your undivided attention, using guilt and jealousy to pull you into their nightmarish world, where their needs are always center stage, and your well-being is but an afterthought.

Detoxing from a Drama Queen

Now, brave soul, let's arm you for the final battle. To cleanse yourself of a Drama Queen's curse, you must first build an emotional fortress—strong and unyielding as the ancient castle walls. Engage with their ghastly tales, but keep your heart guarded, like a knight in shining armor. Set boundaries that are as firm as gravestones and let not their chaos breach your walls of peace.

Remember, Drama Queens feast on your reactions, so starve them of the attention they crave. Let their cries for drama fade into the night, as you encourage them to face their fears without an audience. Establish a sanctuary of calm, a serene refuge from their stormy ways, where you can rest and recharge in peace.

In the end, facing a Drama Queen requires a balance of compassion and steel—acknowledging their cries for attention without losing yourself in their labyrinth of shadows. Keep the drama for the ghostly houses, and craft connections built on trust, respect, and quiet moments of true connection.

Detoxing from a Drama Queen is like stepping out of a ghost story and into the light of day. So, take your seat in the audience, watch the show unfold, but remember—you're no longer part of their twisted script.

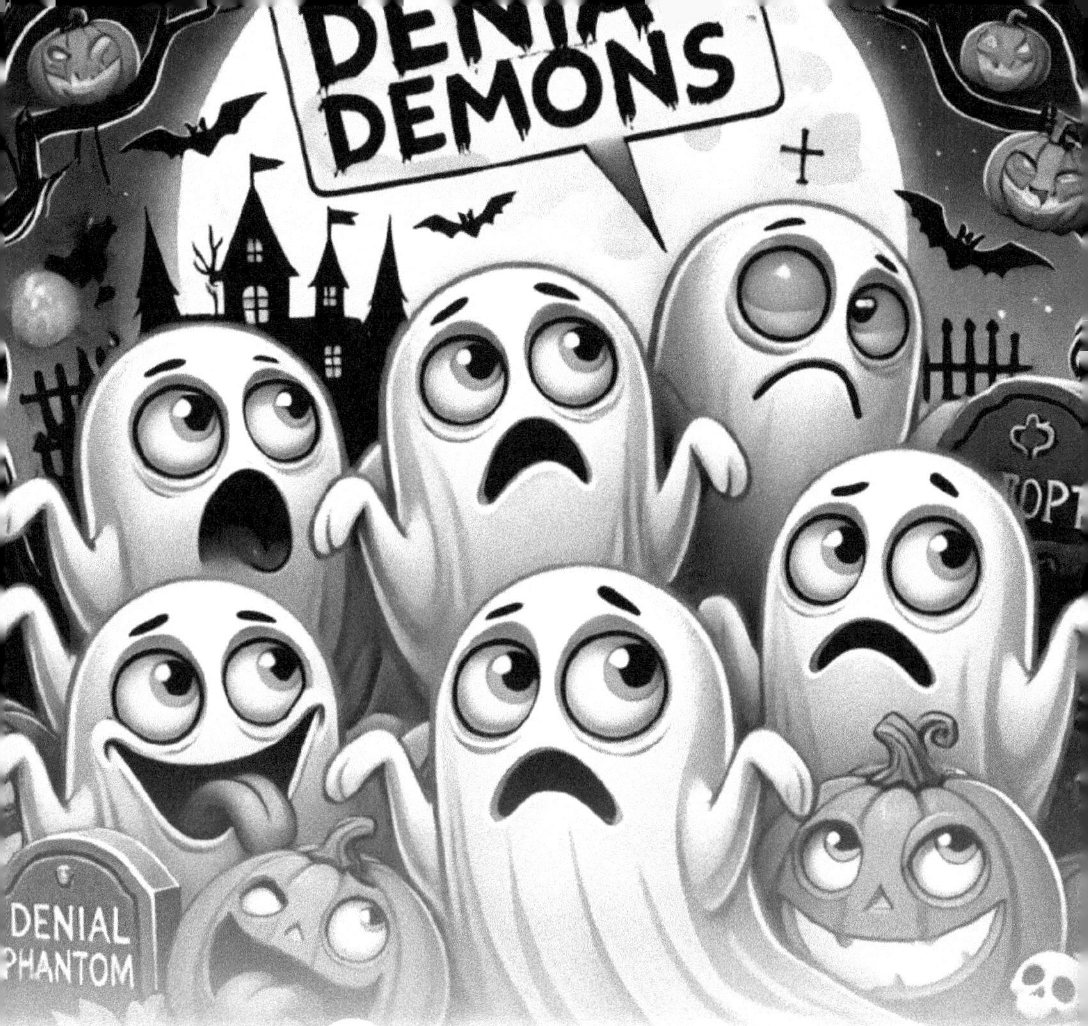

3RD LAIR

Denial Demons

The Relentless Blamers

Beware the Denial Demons—Blamers, those eerie Energy Vampires who haunt the halls of responsibility, forever slipping through the cracks of accountability. Late for work? It's the traffic's curse (never mind the eight times they hit snooze). Bombed that presentation? Blame it on the office's eerie vibes, not their lack of preparation. These unearthly beings are masters of the dark art of finger-pointing, always casting themselves as the innocent victim in their own chilling tales. Beware, for if you find yourself ensnared in their web of excuses, you may soon become their next scapegoat.

As you cross paths with the shadowy world of Denial Demons, they emerge from the misty, emotional fog-like apparitions, eternally cloaked in denial. These entities have perfected the sinister skill of deflection, transforming every encounter into a twisted game where responsibility is a phantom they're always eager to pass on. Their presence chills the air as they weave stories that absolve them of any wrongdoing, leaving them trapped by their own making. In their other-worldly realm, accountability is as foreign as a long-lost spirit, and every problem becomes a cursed artifact they quickly pass on to the nearest unsuspecting soul.

The more you engage with Denial Demons, the more you realize that, in their eyes, nothing is ever truly their fault. They spin elaborate tales, shifting the blame onto others, as if every situation they touch is cursed to spiral into a nightmare of avoidance and accusation. Interacting with them feels like chasing shadows—always elusive, always deflecting, leaving you drained and bewildered.

Masters of Evasion

Imagine a Blamer as a spirit who, with every small mishap, swiftly casts the blame away like a spell, never allowing even a trace of accountability to stick. Engaging with them feels like trying to pin down a phantom—forever elusive, constantly shifting, and always avoiding their own empty reflection. These ghostly figures are masters of deflection, weaving tales that absolve them of any wrongdoing, no matter how small or significant the issue. Whether it's a minor inconvenience like a spilled drink or a major life decision gone awry, they'll always find a way to point their finger at someone else, ensuring they remain the innocent victim in their own shadowy narrative. Their talent lies in their ability to vanish from the scene of responsibility as if they were never there, leaving you to wonder if they were ever truly involved at all.

The Curse of Twisted Celebrations

What should be joyful moments are often transformed into eerie trials under a Denial Demons curse. Celebrations become treks through a forest of accusations and tension, where the joy is drained, and love is twisted into a day of discord. Instead of basking in the glow of shared happiness, you find yourself navigating a minefield of resentments and unspoken grudges, each step fraught with the possibility of triggering yet another blame game. The air becomes thick with mistrust and resentment, trapping everyone in a cycle of defensiveness and shadowy accusations instead of working together to clear the dark clouds overhead. These Blamers have an uncanny ability to turn even the simplest of gatherings into a trial by fire, where every word, every gesture is scrutinized for potential fault, leaving everyone involved drained and disheartened by the end. It's as if they thrive on the discord, drawing energy from the chaos they create, ensuring that no one leaves the encounter unscathed.

Breaking From the Denial Demon Spell

The first step in breaking free from the ghostly grip of a Denial Demon is to recognize the dark influence they've cast over your life. These sinister spirits are masters at weaving webs of deceit, shifting blame with a flick of their hands, leaving you tangled in their shadowy narrative without even realizing it. But you, dear seeker, deserve connections bathed in the light of truth, where mistakes are owned and mended, not used to build walls of resentment.

It's time to reclaim your power, to refuse the role of scapegoat in their endless parade of accusations. By seeing through their tricks and refusing to play the part they've scripted for you, you begin to unravel the threads of their influence. Slowly but surely, you'll break free from the spell they've woven, reclaiming your agency, standing firm in your truth, and banishing the narrative they've tried to trap you in.

Fortifying Against the Shadows

To protect yourself from the Denial Demon's relentless blame, you must lay down boundaries as if drawing a protective circle of salt—clear, firm, and unyielding. These boundaries act as your sacred shield, guarding your spirit from their attempts to pull you into their web of guilt and manipulation. But this isn't just about saying no; it's about reinforcing your own self-worth, ensuring that their shadowy negativity doesn't cloud your reality. Seek out relationships where flaws are admitted under the glow of honesty, not twisted into weapons of despair. In these connections, the journey is one of shared growth, not a one-sided blame game. This is where your soul finds nourishment—in the light of mutual respect, where accountability is a shared responsibility and not a dark tool for manipulation. Here, within these fortified bonds, you stand strong, untouched by the Denial Demon's shadows.

Clearing the Fog of Blame

As you cleanse yourself from the haunting grip of a Denial Demon, remember that detoxing isn't just about banishing negativity; it's about inviting in healthier, more nurturing interactions. These are relationships where both parties can grow, acknowledging imperfections, and celebrating successes hand in hand. It's about transforming the atmosphere from one of mistrust and resentment to one of mutual respect and understanding. This process may involve difficult conversations, setting new expectations, and even letting go of relationships that no longer serve your well-being. But in the end, it's about creating a life where your energy is spent on building positive connections, not defending yourself against unwarranted accusations. The fog of blame lifts, revealing a clearer path forward, one where you can walk with your head held high, free from the shadows of past misunderstandings.

Shadows of the Past

A Denial Demon is like a monster from the past, eternally deflecting blame with eerie precision. They turn every personal failure into an external curse, casting shadows outward, never reflecting on their own dark corners. These shadows stretch back into the past, reaching into every mistake, every setback, and every disappointment, casting them as the work of others rather than the consequences of their own actions. In their lonely world, they are always the victim of some external force, be it a person, circumstance, or even fate itself. This refusal to acknowledge their role in their own life story keeps them trapped in a cycle of bitterness and resentment, unable to move forward, unable to grow. It's as if they are possessed by the ghosts of their own choices, yet refuse to see them, instead projecting these phantoms onto those around them. Recognizing this pattern is crucial for breaking free from their influence, as it allows you to see the truth behind the shadows they cast, freeing yourself from their grasp and reclaiming your power.

Denial Demons on the Creepy Trail of Life

The Perennial Finger-Pointer: Imagine a shadowy figure that lurks in the corners of every conversation, always ready to point their bony finger in someone else's direction. Like a relentless echo in an old, haunted mansion, their refrain is always the same: "It's not my fault!" Whether the soup's too cold or the project fell apart, you can bet they'll find a scapegoat faster than you can say "Boo!" Their presence in your life feels like a never-ending rerun of the same spooky episode—nothing is ever their fault, and the blame always falls on someone else. Trying to hold them accountable is like trying to catch a ghost in a net—elusive and frustrating, leaving you feeling like you're chasing shadows.

The Society Shadowcaster: This Demon cloaks themselves in the uncertainty of the world, using the chaos of society's ills as a smokescreen to dodge personal responsibility. When it comes to friends and family, they're perpetually stifled, trapped in a web of indecision and inaction. Did they forget your birthday? It's because they're overwhelmed by the constant barrage of bad news—who has the mental space for celebrations in such a world? Didn't show up to help when you needed them? Blame it on the uncertainty of the times, with politics and global issues making every decision feel like walking through a minefield.

For them, every missed commitment or ignored responsibility is just another casualty of the world's unpredictability. They hesitate, second-guessing every move, paralyzed by the fear of making the wrong choice in a world where nothing seems certain. Confronting them feels like trying to reach through a thick fog—everything is obscured, and you're left wondering if they'll ever break free from the shadows and take control of their own actions.

The Past-Dweller: This Denial Demon is perpetually troubled by the ghosts of their past. Forever trapped in the cobwebbed corners of their own history, they can't seem to move on from long-gone events. Every conversation feels like stepping into a time warp where past grievances are exhumed and paraded around like restless spirits. Instead of addressing present issues, they summon the relics of what once was, using them as shields against taking responsibility now. The Past-Dweller is more comfortable reliving the past than facing the present, leaving you feeling like you're stuck in a spooky old film reel, looping endlessly through the same scenes of bygone blame.

The Complainer: Envision a storm cloud with a face, perpetually grumbling as it drifts through your life. This blamer demon is enveloped in a perpetual fog of grievance, where every attempt at positivity is smothered by their relentless negativity. Sunshine in their life? They'll grumble about the glare. A good fortune? They'll find the hidden curse. Being around them is like trying to enjoy a sunny day at the graveyard—no matter how hard you try to lift the mood; they're determined to keep things gloomy. Their complaints are like a ghostly chorus that follows you wherever you go, dragging down your spirits with every moan and groan.

The Injustice Collector: This Energy Vampire keeps a ledger like an ancient bookkeeper in a cursed crypt, meticulously tallying every perceived slight and storing them away for future use. You didn't say hello? It's noted. You were late once? It's in the book. They hoard these grievances like cursed treasures, ready to pull them out at a moment's notice, usually when you least expect it. Every interaction with them feels like a step into a eerie archive, where your past mistakes and minor infractions are kept alive like restless spirits, waiting to be unleashed in a future conflict. Their ability to recall these "injustices" with eerie precision makes you feel like you're constantly walking on eggshells, never knowing when the next ghostly grudge will be dragged out into the light.

Detoxing from a Denial Demon

Facing a Denial Demon is like battling a shadowy vampire that refuses to acknowledge its own reflection. The first step in your eerie quest is to not take their tricks personally. These ghouls thrive on twisting reality, but remember, their denial is a reflection of their own fears, not your worth. Set boundaries as if laying down a protective circle of salt, defining clearly where your tolerance ends, and your self-respect begins. Let them know that the fog they cast won't obscure the truth forever.

Moving forward together requires conjuring an environment where accountability shines like a glowing jack-o'-lantern in the night, illuminating the path out of their murky grasp. But beware—detoxing from a Denial Demon may require you to step back, creating a buffer of space to breathe freely, far from their haunting grip.

As you retreat into the safety of your enchanted circle, surround yourself with allies who mirror the growth and positivity you seek. These are the spirits of your support, helping you fortify your defenses against the dark pull of denial. With their help, you can step out of the shadows and into a brighter, healthier relational light, leaving the Denial Demon to wrestle with its own reflection in the dark.

Wailing Spirits

The Wannabe Whiners

Beware the Wailing Spirits, the Wannabe Whiners—those souls who drift in the shadows of their own perceived inadequacies, forever troubled by the successes of others. These phantoms of envy move through life with a constant sense of longing, always eclipsed by the bright, blazing trails of those around them. They dwell in a twilight world, where their own dimly lit paths seem pale and insignificant compared to the achievements of others.

For the Wannabe Whiners, every milestone reached by a friend, every accolade won by a colleague, is not a source of inspiration but a bitter reminder of their own unmet potential. Trapped in a loop of self-doubt and jealousy, their spirits are weighed down by the heavy chains of comparison and insecurity. Interacting with them can feel like wandering through a foggy, creepy forest where the light of success is always out of reach, and every step forward is met with the cold grasp of envy.

These Energy Vampires are the eternal underdogs, tethered to a soul who perpetually casts themselves as the dark horse, a background figure in their own haunting tale. No matter the conversation, they are always one step behind, their spirit dampened by the constant rain of others' achievements. It's as if they're adrift on a foggy lake, endlessly rowing in circles, never reaching the shore of self-satisfaction.

Jealousy drifts into every gathering with a Wailing Spirits, casting a chill over what should be moments of shared joy. Each story of success becomes a shadow at their feast, whispering of what they lack. Participating in celebrations with them feels like walking through a ghostly hall, where every cheer and laughter echoes with a hint of their discontent.

Trying to lift their spirits is like lighting a candle in a drafty crypt—the flame flickers weakly, fighting against the damp, heavy air of their negativity. No matter how much warmth or encouragement you offer, their shadows only grow longer, deepening with each attempt. It's a draining dance, where instead of basking in the glow of shared happiness, you find yourself pulled into their murky depths, where your light struggles to pierce the gloom.

Identifying the Wailing Spirits

The Achievement Dampener: You share the thrilling news of your promotion, expecting your friend to join in your excitement. But instead of celebrating, they respond with a sigh, lamenting how they're always trapped in the shadows, never catching a break. Your moment of joy is quickly eclipsed by the gloom they cast, like a cloud passing over the full moon.

The Praise Deflector: Someone compliments them on a small victory, but they immediately downplay it, insisting it was nothing special. They quickly pivot to lament about how they've never achieved anything truly meaningful, pulling the conversation into a shadowy pit of self-pity, where praise is swallowed whole.

The Self-Absorber: During a chat about a recent adventure, instead of sharing in your excitement, they bring up how they've never had the chance to experience anything like it. Their envy creeps into the conversation like a chilly breeze, leaving you feeling guilty for enjoying the light while they dwell in the darkness.

The Opportunity Overlooker: When discussing future plans, they're quick to point out the obstacles, speaking as if cursed never to see the light of success. Even when you offer solutions, they dismiss them with a wave, preferring to stay wrapped in their shroud of missed chances, like a ghost bound to the regrets of the past.

Detoxing from a Wailing Spirit

Dealing with a Wailing Spirit isn't just about managing their constant envy; it's about resisting their attempts to spread that envy like a creeping fog on a cold, dark night. These spirits thrive on playing the perpetual underdog, cloaking themselves in a shroud of self-pity while drawing others into their web of dissatisfaction. Their endless comparisons and mournful sighs are a kind of emotional sorcery, casting a shadow over your triumphs while amplifying their own sense of inadequacy. It's a spell that can leave you feeling drained, your own successes dimmed by the shadows they cast.

Breaking free from the grip of a Wailing Spirit is like shattering a spell cast on a moonless night. You must recognize that you can't be their eternal guiding light, forever illuminating their path while they refuse to find their own way out of the darkness. Encourage them to ignite their own torches, to find joy in their achievements without casting shadows over others. This might mean setting firm boundaries—drawing a circle of salt around yourself, a protective barrier that keeps their restless energy at bay. By maintaining a healthy distance, you allow them the space to discover their strength, freeing you to walk your path unburdened by their ghostly presence.

Remember, you are not their keeper. Your journey is your own, and while you can offer a flicker of light to guide them, it's up to them to step out of their own shadows. Protect your energy, and don't let their eerie laments or ceaseless comparisons dim your own bright glow. In the end, your light is meant to shine on your own path, not be absorbed by those who refuse to escape their own darkness.

Cauldron Crawlers

The Ghastly Grip of the Clingy Crabs

Picture a cauldron bubbling under the eerie glow of the moon, not filled with a witch's brew, but crawling with crabs. As one daring crab tries to escape, the others reach out with their clawed limbs, dragging it back into the depths. Now, imagine this unsettling scene playing out in your own life with certain friends, family members, or coworkers. These are the clingy critters, driven by their own shadows of insecurity, determined to pull you back into their gloomy comfort zone whenever you attempt to climb out.

The Curse of the Crab Bucket

On your journey of discovery, the Cauldron Crawlers creep in like a thick, chilling fog. Just as you're about to step into the light of a new achievement—be it a career leap, a newfound passion, or a surge of self-confidence—these shadowy figures emerge, ready to yank you back into the darkness. It's chilling: you share your triumph, expecting cheers, only to receive a murmur, "Are you sure you're ready for this?" Their intent isn't just to keep you grounded; it's to anchor you alongside them in the murky waters of their own insecurities.

Dancing with Crabs

Dealing with these clingy critters is like dancing in a crab bucket—they're always scuttling just out of step, gripping onto you with their sharp claws, holding you back every time you try to break free. These crabs aren't malevolent beings; they're afraid, terrified of being left behind as you climb out of the bucket, seeking brighter shores beyond their dark, familiar waters. They fear change and the unknown, so they cling to what they know—dragging you down with them in the process.

As much as you care for these crabs, their fears become heavy chains, anchoring both of you to the murky depths of complacency. Every attempt you make to rise is met with a desperate tug, pulling you back into the shadows, preventing you from reaching the surface where the light of growth and progress awaits. It's a dance that can leave you feeling trapped, with every step forward met by a forceful pull backward, keeping you entangled in the gloomy depths.

To truly break free, you'll need to understand their fears without letting them become your own, finding the strength to unchain yourself from their grasp and rise above the shadows of the bucket.

The Haunting Crab Tug-of-War

Every time you inch closer to the light of new opportunities, it feels like you're caught in a crab's relentless grip, pulling you back into the murky depths of past complacencies. These clingy critters spin tales of caution, casting shadows over your ambitions and chilling your progress with their cold, unyielding claws. Just the thought of you advancing sends them into a frenzy, triggering a desperate panic that compels them to drag you back into the dark, familiar graveyard of old habits and stagnant dreams.

It's a relentless tug-of-war, where your every move toward growth is met with a forceful yank, pulling you back into the crab bucket's gloomy confines. Their grip tightens with each step you take, their fears manifesting as chains that bind you to the very shadows you're trying to escape. It's as if they can't bear to see you rise, so they do everything in their power to keep you tethered to the bottom, lost in the crypt of what once was, rather than what could be.

How to recognize Cauldron Crawlers

The Skeptical Snapper: This crab sulks in the shadows, quick to dismiss your aspirations with a chilling snap of its claws. Every time you share a new idea or ambition, the Skeptical Snapper is there, ready to cast a sinister doubt over your dreams. "Are you really sure about this?" it hisses, sowing seeds of uncertainty just when you're ready to leap into the unknown. They're so traumatized by their own fears that they can't fathom anyone escaping the cauldron's grip. Their skepticism clings to you like a ghostly chain, pulling you back into the murky depths.

The Overprotective Pincher: This crab believes it's keeping you safe by trapping you in its grasp, warning of the perils that lie beyond the cauldron's edge. Every time you inch closer to the light, the Overprotective Pincher tightens its grip, whispering, "It's too risky out there." Their intentions aren't wicked; they're possessed by the fear of losing you to the unknown. Yet, their constant pinching anchors you in the dark, cold waters of caution, preventing you from venturing into the brighter, moonlit shores that beckon.

The Envious Claw: Green with envy, this crab's claws are sharp and relentless, driven by jealousy that festers in the shadows. Each time you achieve something new, the Envious Claw emerges, tugging at your ankles, desperate to pull you back into the cauldron's depths. Your success shines a harsh light on their own stagnation, stirring their envy into a fog that clouds your triumphs. Their jealousy is like a mist that creeps in, making you question whether it's worth trying to escape the cauldron's dark embrace at all.

The Nostalgic Nipper: This crab is trapped in the past, clinging to the remnants of what once was. "Remember the good old days?" it murmurs, nipping at your heels, trying to pull you back into the familiar darkness. The Nostalgic Nipper fears the unknown so much that it becomes a phantom of the past, keeping you shackled in a loop of memories. It's not that they don't care about your growth; they simply can't let go of what's been lost, keeping you ensnared in a time long gone, instead of moving toward what could be.

The Dependent Dragger: This crab relies on you to stay afloat, its claws ever reaching to pull you back whenever you try to escape the cauldron's depths. They fear that if you rise, they'll be left alone in the dark waters, and so they drag you down with them, time and time again. The Dependent Dragger isn't evil; they're frightened by the terror of being left behind. But their dependence becomes a heavy shackle, dragging you into the abyss every time you reach for the light. To break free from their grip means risking their wrath or sorrow, but it's the only way to find your path out of the cauldron's cursed waters.

Breaking the Crab's Curse

Escaping the clutches of these clingy critters requires more than just a simple push—it demands a spell of protection, a circle of power that no crab can cross. These crabs, with their relentless claws and shadowy games, thrive on pulling you back into the depths, but with the right incantations, you can break free from their curse.

First, set your boundaries as if you were laying down a ring of salt—an unbreakable line that wards off their dark influence. When they attempt their usual tricks, do not engage in their drama. Instead, calmly assert your own reality: "I see your shadowy games, but I won't join your dance." This is your protective charm, a way to maintain your strength without succumbing to their grasp.

Building this emotional fortress isn't about banishing them into the void; it's about safeguarding your own spirit, ensuring that your energy isn't constantly drained by their fears and insecurities. True companionship is a shared journey, where both souls can grow together, not a one-sided tug-of-war that leaves you exhausted and empty.

Encourage these crabs to face their own fears, to find their own source of joy and light. Perhaps, with time, they will see that the shadows they cling to are merely illusions, and that they too can emerge into a brighter, more fulfilling existence. By doing so, you not only protect yourself but also offer them a chance to escape the cauldron's dark curse.

Remember, breaking free from the crab's curse doesn't mean abandoning those you care about—it means refusing to let their fears anchor you in the dark. Together, you might just step out of the shadows and into the light, unburdened by the chains that once held you back.

6TH LAIR

Gloom Mongers

Victim Pity Party

Imagine this chilling scenario: Each day unfurls like a spooky re-run of the same grim tale. The Gloom Monger, a quintessential Victim-type Energy Vampire, perpetually lingers at the heart of some melodrama or misfortune. In this endless ghost story, they cast themselves as the hapless victim, while those around them are summoned time and again to lift their spirits or resolve their ceaseless calamities.

It's as though you have tuned into a celestial frequency, one that alerts you to every minor mishap in their life. Missed the bus? To them, it's a catastrophe akin to a cursed caravan vanishing into the night. Spilled their potion? An absolute tragedy, as if the elixir of life itself has been lost forever. They possess an uncanny knack for transforming molehills into mountains of horror—and those nearby are expected to scale these eerie heights. Your role goes far beyond mere bystander; you become their lifeline, perpetually tethered to their crises.

These Gloom Mongers have perfected the dark art of eternal suffering, spinning woeful tales with the skill of seasoned spell-casters, always portraying themselves as the tormented souls caught in an endless loop of misfortune and woe. They conjure sympathy with every sigh and lament, expertly manipulating those around them into roles of caretakers or problem-solvers, ensnaring others in their web of wails.

As the days turn into nights and the seasons pass like shadows, anyone caught in their orbit may find themselves exhausted, drained by the weight of their unrelenting despair. The Gloom Monger knows no rest, and neither do those trapped in their tale of woe—a story that repeats itself with chilling consistency, leaving everyone wondering if there's any escape from their cold, calculated grasp.

In this haunting dynamic, you're left exhausted, feeling as though all your efforts vanish into an abyss. The friendship or relationship morphs into an endless therapy session or a caretaking saga rather than a genuine partnership. It becomes a tale of one-sided emotional labor, with you continuously giving and them endlessly taking, leaving you drained by the imbalance.

Unmasking the Gloom Mongers

The Constant Complainer: This ghostly figure has a PhD in complaining. Everything's always wrong—the weather's too spooky, their job's too cursed, their coffee's too cold. Every chat with them turns into a vent session, and you're stuck being a cheerleader in their carnival, offering solutions that never seem to stick. It's like pouring your energy into a bottomless pit, and boy, is it draining. The more you try to soothe their woes, the more they conjure up new grievances, leaving you feeling like you're caught in an endless loop of their dark, stormy weather.

The Eternal Raincloud: Picture this—you're basking in the glow of a splendid day, but your companion? They possess an uncanny talent for summoning dark clouds even on the sunniest afternoons. Their world is one of endless doom and gloom, casting a pall over every attempt to brighten their spirits. Trying to bring some light into their life feels like pushing a cursed boulder up forested hill, exhausting and futile. No matter how bright your lantern shines, they'll snuff it out, leaving you to wonder if it's you who's lost in their shadowy, never-ending night.

The Drama Magnet: Some souls draw drama like vampires to blood, don't they? If you find yourself ensnared by a Victim Drama Magnet, you're no stranger to the chaos they conjure. Every moment with them is a new disaster—a missed call morphs into a ghostly tale, a lost item becomes a cursed relic—and guess who's cast as the hero in their never-ending spooky saga? That's right, it's you. The relentless demands of their supernatural crises leave you drained, as their life plays out like a continuous horror show, with you stuck cleaning up the eerie aftermath.

The Sinister Puppeteer: Beware the Gloom Monger, a master of manipulation who knows just how to pull your heartstrings like a puppeteer in a dark, cursed theater. With an arsenal of "remember when I…" and "my life is so tough because…" they ensnare you in a web of guilt, making you feel as if you owe them the world. It's a sinister trap, slowly dragging you into a pit of quicksand, where each step deeper binds you tighter in their suffocating, guilt-ridden embrace. The harder you try to escape, the more you find yourself gasping for breath in their relentless grip.

Victim Pity Party: A twisted masquerade where each player wears a mask of woe, and you're the only one without a disguise. They lure you into their macabre dance, siphoning your energy as you struggle to meet their endless demands for attention and sympathy. But remember, this is their haunting ball, and you're not required to join the dance. Let their eerie tunes play out without you—don't let their sorrowful masquerade draw you into its endless, draining waltz.

The Refreshing Escape From Gloom Mongers

Escaping the clutches of a Gloom Monger is like breaking free from a cursed tale where you're always cast as the reluctant savior. These shadowy figures weave webs of never-ending drama, pulling you into their cluttered world as their eternal rescuer. But here is the chilling truth: you're not bound to be their constant hero, always solving their ghostly problems or bearing their heavy burdens.

Envision yourself constructing enchanted walls around your energy, as unyielding as the gates of a haunted mansion. When they begin to spin their tales of woe, listen if you must, but don't be pulled into their bubbling cauldron of chaos. Encourage them to confront their own shadows, to take responsibility for their lives. And if, after setting these boundaries, they persist in clinging to their role as the eternal victim, it may be time to mount your broomstick and soar away, leaving their eerie grip behind as you reclaim your peace.

7TH LAIR

Shadow Controller

Welcome to the eerie realm of the Shadow Controller—a ghastly figure lurking in the darkened corridors of life, tightening the strings and pulling you deeper into their web of control. These Energy Vampires aren't content with just managing their own existence; they seek to dominate yours as well, turning every shared moment into a scene from their meticulously crafted horror script. If you're on a quest to banish toxic forces from your life, beware! The Shadow Controller may be hiding in the shadows, ready to sink their claws into your every decision.

This Energy Vampire thrives on fear, aggression, and manipulation, feeding off the power they gain from belittling, threatening, and pushing others around. Often targeting those they perceive as weaker; the Controller's interactions are marked by a chilling lack of empathy and an insatiable need to assert their superiority. They might cloak their behavior in the guise of "tough love" or claim they're just being "honest," but their true motive is to maintain control and keep others off balance. By creating a constant atmosphere of tension and anxiety, they drain your energy, leaving you feeling powerless and insecure. Over time, their relentless aggression can erode your self-esteem, making it increasingly difficult to stand up for yourself or break free from their toxic grip.

The Controller's Grip on Your Life

Imagine being trapped in a haunted carriage with someone who insists on holding the reins, guiding your every move through the foggy night. The Controller isn't just a backseat driver; they've taken over the entire carriage, dictating not just the direction but also the pace, the stops, and even the eerie soundtrack. These ghouls believe they hold the only map to the truth, and woe to you if you dare suggest an alternative route.

Entangling yourself with a Controller is like living under a ghostly microscope. They scrutinize your every choice; from the clothes you wear to the thoughts that dare cross your mind. It's as if you're walking a tightrope strung across a bottomless pit, where one wrong step earns you a lecture on how you should've done it their way. The constant criticism and control make you feel as though your every move is being watched, judged, and found wanting. Over time, this can drain the life out of you, leaving you feeling like a shadow of your former self.

The Many Masks of the Controller

Controllers are shapeshifters, donning various masks to maintain their grip on your life. Here are some of the ghostly guises they might wear:

The Micromanager Taskmaster: This Energy Vampire has an eye for detail—sinister, obsessive detail. They want to oversee every aspect of your life, from how you fold your sheets to the friends you invite into your haunted house. Living under the gaze of a Micromanager feels like being under a constant magnifying glass, where nothing you do ever escapes their watchful, critical eye. The relentless scrutiny can leave you feeling smothered, as if you're trapped in a glass jar, with no room to breathe or grow.

The Opinion Enforcer: Beware of this ghost who believes their opinions are carved in ancient stone. To them, the world is a place of absolutes—black and white, right and wrong. In their eyes, your thoughts are mere shadows unless they align perfectly with theirs. The Opinion Enforcer seeks to reshape your mind, leaving little room for your own individuality to haunt. Over time, their constant undermining of your ideas can erode your confidence, making you doubt your own judgment and silencing your voice.

The Planner: Ah, the Planner—this vampire abhors spontaneity. Every moment of your life must be meticulously planned, from moonlit strolls to the distant future. While a little organization can be beneficial, the Planner's rigid script leaves no room for your ideas. Any deviation from their plan can lead to conflict, or worse, they might dismiss your ideas as mere ghost stories. Living with a Planner can make you feel stifled, as if you're constantly being herded into a narrow path with no room to explore your own dreams.

How They Attract the Kind-Hearted and Vulnerable

Controllers often attract those with kind hearts and low self-esteem—those who are eager to please, who doubt their own worth, and who are more likely to bend under pressure. They prey on the compassionate, drawing them in with a mix of charm and intimidation. At first, their take-charge attitude might seem like a relief, a guiding hand in the darkness. But soon, the kind-hearted find themselves trapped, their good nature exploited as the Controller tightens their grip, feeding off their need for approval and making them feel even smaller.

For those already struggling with self-esteem, the Controller's dominance can seem almost comforting, as if they're taking the burden of decision-making off your shoulders. But this is a cruel illusion—the more you give in, the more they take, until there's nothing left of your confidence, only the hollow echoes of their demands.

Living Under the Controller's Watchful Eye

Being ensnared by a Controller can feel like you're living under constant scrutiny. Every choice you make must pass through their approval. Imagine your life as a scary movie, and there's this ghost who insists on directing every scene, leaving you with little room to breathe.

Reclaiming Your Spirit

Breaking free from the clutches of a Controller is like escaping the grip of a cursed puppet master. It's time to snatch back your identity and ensure that your relationships are built on mutual respect and eerie freedom. You're not some wandering soul in search of completion—you're a whole, spirited being with a ghostly glow all your own. What you need is a fellow traveler on this journey, not someone trying to seize the reins of your broomstick.

As the Halloween fog rolls in and shadows deepen, be on the lookout for the Controller lurking in the dark corners, ready to ensnare you in their web. But remember—you hold the power to sever those threads of control. Embrace your own chilling narrative, let the Controller's hold fade into the swirling mist, and take your rightful place as the lead actor in your own tale. After all, it's your story to tell, and it's time you stepped into the eerie spotlight.

THE 8TH LAIR

The Chronic Critic

An Energy Vampire with a Thousand Gripes

Imagine this: You're trying to carve out a little peace and positivity in your life, perhaps light a few candles to ward off the dark. Just as you're getting comfortable in your cozy nook of self-assurance, the Chronic Critic swoops in with a harsh word or a disapproving glare.

This isn't just about the occasional nitpick; it's a relentless haunting, where every action is scrutinized, and no good deed goes unpunished. The Critic doesn't want to see you grow; it thrives on keeping you tethered to self-doubt, feeding off the energy that drains from you each time you're told you're not good enough. Over time, the once-warm friendship or relationship turns cold, the atmosphere thick with the icy breath of relentless criticism.

Spotting the Chronic Critic

That shadowy specter lurking in the corners of your mind, whispering its chilling incantations to keep you shackled in self-doubt. Do you ever feel like you're under a dark enchantment, where no matter how hard you try, it's never quite enough? That's the Chronic Critic casting its wicked spell, eager to feast on your insecurities and trap you in a crypt of unworthiness. This ghastly figure takes on many forms, each more sinister than the last, and if you're not careful, it will drain your spirit dry.

The Nitpicker: Beware the Nitpicker, a ghostly ghoul with eyes that pierce through the veil of perfection to find the tiniest flaws. It's as if they wield a cursed magnifying glass, forever focusing on the minute, insignificant details no one else notices. Their nitpicks cling to you like cobwebs in a haunted house, tangling you in a web of anxiety, always dreading the next flaw they'll find. Living with the Nitpicker is like being trapped in a labyrinth of mirrors, each one reflecting a distorted version of yourself, never quite right, never quite enough.

The "Never Good Enough" Menace: This relentless vampire thrives on your exhaustion, always setting the bar just out of reach. Imagine climbing a cursed hill that grows steeper with every step—no matter how hard you strive, the peak is always a shadowy illusion, just beyond your grasp. This menace whispers in your ear, "Almost there," but the path keeps winding, leaving you in a perpetual state of striving, never arriving. It's as if you're cursed to wander an endless forest of unattainable goals, where every effort is swallowed by the darkness.

The "Honesty Brutalist": Beware the Brutalist, a spirit who hides behind the mask of 'just being honest,' yet their words cut sharper than a witch's curse. They claim their truth is a guiding light, but it's really a cold wind that chills your very soul, leaving you shivering in the night. Their 'honesty' dismisses your feelings as mere ghostly whispers, unworthy of consideration. This spectral figure uses the guise of truth to keep you in line, always reminding you of your place in their dark hierarchy, where your worth is but a flickering candle in a drafty old mansion.

The Underminer: Cloaked in concern and disguised as a friend, this is the most cunning of all. They plant seeds of doubt with a smile, casting long shadows over your confidence. "Are you sure about that?" they'll ask, their voice dripping with the venom of a well-placed curse. Their words are like whispers carried on a ghostly breeze, filling your mind with fog and uncertainty. Before long, you're stumbling through a graveyard of second-guessing, unsure of your own decisions, as if every step could be your last.

The Guilt Tripper: A vampire who feasts on your joy, draining the life from your successes with their heavy chains of guilt. Just when you begin to bask in the light of your achievements, they remind you of their suffering, casting a shadow over your happiness. It's as if your joy is a cursed object, something that should never be fully enjoyed without the weight of their misery. Their words wrap around you like a chain forged in the fires of regret, pulling you back into the darkness whenever you try to step into the light.

These insidious spirits may haunt your thoughts, but remember, you hold the power to break their curse. Shine the lantern of self-awareness on these phantoms, challenge their whispers with your own truth, and reclaim your spirit from their icy grip. In the end, these shadowy figures are nothing more than echoes in the dark—smoke and mirrors that dissolve when faced with the light of your inner strength. So, arm yourself with kindness, wield the sword of self-love, and banish these Chronic Critics to the netherworld where they belong.

Living Under the Chronic Critic's Gaze

Being spooked by a Chronic Critic in your friendships and relationships is like being trapped in a funhouse of mirrors, but instead of reflections, you see distortions. Every flaw is magnified, every mistake spotlighted, and the light of your achievements dims to a mere flicker. You're constantly under the Critic's gaze, feeling their icy breath on your neck, quick to point out what you did wrong but slow—oh so slow—to celebrate your successes. This constant scrutiny creates an environment where fear of failure overshadows any joy in your accomplishments, trapping you in a cycle of anxiety and self-doubt.

The Exorcism: Banishing the Chronic Critic

It's time to turn the tables and confront this ghastly presence. Start by reinforcing your defenses—boost your self-esteem and remember your worth. The Critic's harsh words are nothing more than ghostly echoes of their own insecurities. Have a heart-to-heart with this spirit, letting them know how their words slice through you like a cursed blade. Draw your lines in the sand—what you're willing to tolerate and what is simply off-limits. If they can't respect that, it may be time to consider whether you're living with a ghost or a friend.

Banishing the Chronic Critic isn't just about warding off negativity—it's about reclaiming your castle, brick by brick, with walls fortified by self-love and a moat filled with self-worth. Understand that constructive feedback is one thing, but constant criticism is another beast altogether. You deserve friendships and relationships that lift you up, not ones that drag you down into the crypt. Here's to finding companions who celebrate your strengths, support you through your weaknesses, and banish the ghostly shadows that once followed your every step.

So, as you walk through the eclectic halls of your friendships and relationships, keep an eye out for the Chronic Critic. If it appears, you'll know what to do—grab your torch, light up the darkness, and banish that spirit back to the shadows where it belongs. Let the warmth of self-assurance fill the spaces where the Critic once roamed and enjoy the peace that comes with reclaiming your own ghostly tale.

The Deceptive Gaslighter

Welcome to the shadowy domain of the Deceptive Gaslighter—a master of psychological manipulation who thrives on distorting reality and making you question your own sanity. These Energy Vampires are subtle but deadly, weaving their web of lies and deceit so intricately that you may not even realize you're ensnared until it's too late.

Whether they're a partner, friend, or family member, Gaslighters take pleasure in making you doubt your perceptions, memories, and even your very sense of self. They twist the truth until it's unrecognizable, leaving you stranded in a fog of confusion and self-doubt, as if you're wandering through a forest with no clear path of escape.

Spotting the Deceptive Gaslighter

The Shadow of Doubt: In the dim corners of your life, the Deceptive Gaslighter is cloaked in the guise of a concerned friend or family member, weaving their spell of doubt under the color of care. This figure plants seeds of uncertainty, casting shadows over your every move with phrases like, "Are you sure about that?" or "I don't think that's a good idea." It's a slow, creeping curse—each seemingly innocent remark chips away at your confidence, leaving you questioning your instincts. The Underminer's goal is to make you doubt yourself so thoroughly that you become dependent on their guidance, never realizing they're the ones leading you deeper into the shadows of self-doubt.

The Reality Rewriter: Twisting the threads of truth, this vampire has a sinister gift for bending reality until it's unrecognizable, turning your world upside down in the process. They'll deny things they've said or done, or worse, claim you have done things you know you haven't. They rewrite the past, insisting events unfolded differently than you remember, making you doubt your memory and your sanity. This phantom thrives on chaos, creating a world where the past shifts like the walls of a haunted house, leaving you trapped in a reality where nothing is as it seems.

The Narrative Weaver: In the mysterious realm of control, this Energy Vampire is a master Gaslighter, spinning a web of deception so tight that you begin to lose sight of what's real. They dismiss your concerns with a chilling, "You're just being paranoid," or "You're too sensitive," casting doubt on your every emotion. Over time, this constant dismissal erodes your self-esteem, leaving you feeling like a ghost wandering through a story where your voice is lost, and only their version of events matters. The Narrative Weaver's ultimate aim is to control the tale, ensuring that their script is the only one that's told.

The Deflector: The masters of shifting deflection, this Gaslighter wields blame like a cursed artifact, using sleight of hand to avoid taking responsibility for their actions. When confronted, they'll twist the situation, making it seem like you're the one at fault. They deflect with phrases like, "You're making a big deal out of nothing," or "Why are you always so dramatic?" Their game is to keep you off-balance, never realizing they're the puppet master pulling the strings from the shadows. The Deflector's goal is to avoid accountability at all costs, leaving you questioning your reactions and feeling trapped in their web of deceit.

The Doubt Whisperer: Chipping away at your confidence this Energy Vampire haunts your thoughts, subtly eroding your self-esteem, one whisper at a time. They frame their barbs as "just trying to help," but their words carry the weight of a curse. They might say, "I'm only saying this because I care," while implying that you're not capable of handling your own life. Over time, these seemingly insignificant comments accumulate, casting long shadows over your sense of self-worth, leaving you feeling like you're wandering through a haunted house, where every creak is a reminder of your perceived shortcomings.

Deceptive Gaslighter Detox

The sinister Deceptive Gaslighter, a master of illusions, who thrives in the murky shadows of manipulation, twisting your reality until it feels like you're trapped in an endless nightmare. But fear not, for your journey of detoxification begins with awakening from this dark spell and reclaiming your own truth.

Step One: Trust your instincts, those inner whispers that the Gaslighter has tried so hard to drown out. Remember, the reality they've spun is nothing more than a trick of the light—a dark enchantment meant to confuse and control. Cast your protective circle strong and true, fortifying your mind against their distortions. Let no one twist your truth or make you doubt your own sanity.

Step Two: Rebuilding your confidence is like gathering the scattered pieces of your shattered mirror, each reflecting your true self. Surround yourself with allies—your coven of supportive souls—who see you clearly and stand by your side as you reclaim your reality. These wise ones are your lanterns in the darkness, illuminating the path back to self-trust and guiding you out of the foggy forest of doubt that the Gaslighter has conjured.

Step Three: If the Gaslighter's grip continues to tighten, refusing to release you from their twisted web, it may be time to take a brave step away from their toxic influence. Whether they are a so-called friend, a family member, or a partner, reclaim your narrative and distance yourself from their shadowy presence. Your story is yours alone—do not let anyone else wield the pen that writes your destiny.

Step Four: Finally, reflect on the eerie lessons this haunting experience has etched into your soul. Recognize the red flags that appeared in the Gaslighter's spell book and vow to trust your own reality moving forward. You are not a puppet dangling on someone else's strings; you are the author of your own tale, the master of your own fate. Embrace the clarity that comes with breaking free from the Gaslighter's grip and step boldly into the light of your own truth.

You've danced with the darkness and emerged victorious, dear seeker. Now, go forth with your newfound wisdom and let no one ever cloud your reality again.

10TH LAIR

Toxic Gossips

In the dark corners of gatherings and social circles, the Toxic Gossips can be found, weaving webs of deceit and half-truths. These Toxic Gossips aren't content with merely observing; they're driven by an insidious desire to spread whispers that echo through the halls, turning peace into chaos. Their whispered words are like the cold winds that rustle through the leaves in a forest—subtle yet chilling, carrying tales that may or may not hold a shred of truth. The Whispering Shadows aims to keep everyone on edge, creating an environment where trust is fragile, and betrayal is always lurking just out of sight.

The Masks They Wear

The Drama Conjurers: Stirring the cauldron, the Toxic Gossips take great pleasure in stirring the truth, ensuring the brew of discord is always bubbling. They thrive on the chaos their words create casting spells of suspicion and doubt wherever they go. A simple comment is twisted, a harmless action is reimagined, and before you know it, friendships and connections are strained under the weight of their fabrications. These conjurers of chaos aren't just sharing information—they're molding it, shaping it into something dark and twisted, all for the thrill of watching the fallout.

The Reputation Haunters: These Toxic Gossips are like ghosts haunting the reputation of their targets, forever spreading tales that cling to their victims like cobwebs in an abandoned house. The Reputation Haunters delight in tarnishing the names of others, casting doubt and suspicion that sticks even when there's no truth to their words. They operate under the cover of concern, sharing their venomous whispers under the guise of "just wanting to warn you." But their true intention is to see the light dim in their target's eyes, as the weight of slander pulls them deeper into the shadows of social ruin.

The Web Weavers: Trapping you in their threads, they are masters of entanglement, ensnaring their listeners in a sticky web of half-truths and outright lies. They spread their toxic gossip with calculated precision, ensuring that every thread they spin connects to someone else, pulling more and more people into their web. The more tangled the web, the more power they feel, as they watch those around them struggle to extricate themselves from the rumors and falsehoods they've been drawn into. The Web Weavers' goal is to be at the center of this network, where they can pull the strings and watch the drama unfold.

The Shadow Puppeteers: These Energy Vampires don't just spread rumors—they manipulate the very narrative of social interactions, ensuring that their version of events is the one that sticks. They carefully choose what to share and what to withhold, crafting stories that paint themselves in the best light while casting others into shadow. With each word they whisper, they guide the actions and thoughts of those around them, ensuring that their control over the social landscape remains unchallenged. The Shadow Puppeteers aren't just spreading gossip—they're writing the script for everyone else's part in their dark drama.

Detoxing from the Toxic Gossips

Breaking free from the grip of Toxic Gossips requires a keen eye and a steady heart. The first step is to recognize the power of their whispers—don't let their words take root in your mind. Set firm boundaries, refusing to participate in their dark tales or spread their poison further. Confront the Gossip if necessary, shining a light on their behavior and refusing to be drawn into their web. Surround yourself with those who value truth and loyalty, people who will stand by your side even when the shadows of slander loom large. Remember, the Gossip's power fades when their words fall on deaf ears. Protect your energy and let the Toxic Gossips' whispers fade into the night, lost in the darkness where they belong.

11ᵀᴴ LAIR

The Needy Ones

The Bottomless Pit of Demand

In the dim, echoing corridors of your connections, The Needy Ones lurk—always seeking attention, validation, and reassurance. These Energy Vampires latch on like phantoms, drawing from your emotional reserves as if they were an endless well. But beware! The more they take, the more they need, creating a bottomless pit of longing that can never be truly filled. Their insatiable appetite for comfort and guidance drains the life force of those around them, leaving behind a trail of exhaustion and weariness.

Discovering their Vortex

Dragging You into the Depths: The Needy Ones who seem to pull you deeper into their emotional abyss with every encounter. They're constantly in need of advice, support, or just a willing ear to listen to their endless lamentations. Being around them is like trying to swim while tethered to a heavy weight—no matter how hard you struggle to stay afloat; they drag you down into the murky waters of their insecurities. It's a draining dance, always offering a lifeline, knowing that no matter how much you give, it will never be enough to pull them out of their depths.

Craving the Light of Approval: Validation Seekers are those lost souls who crave the flickering light of approval, always fishing for compliments and reassurance to affirm their worth. They return time and again, drawn like moths to the flame of your approval, but it never seems to be enough. Engaging with them feels like stoking a fire that refuses to die out, as they keep coming back for more, trying to keep their fragile self-esteem from crumbling into the shadows.

The Reassurance Hunters: Lost in the fog of doubt, these are the ones who wander in a constant fog of doubt, always questioning their decisions, actions, and even their own worth. They turn to you repeatedly, seeking reassurance that they're on the right path, that they've made the right choices, that they're not lost in the night. But no matter how many times you offer your support, their doubt lingers like a ghostly presence, never fully dispelled. Their need for constant reassurance can become overwhelming, as you find yourself endlessly repeating the same comforting words, hoping that this time, they'll finally take hold.

The People Pleasers: Trapped in the shadow of validation, people pleasers are giving endlessly, not out of pure generosity, but out of a desperate need for validation. They don't yet know their own worth, so they seek it in the approval of others, bending over backward to meet everyone else's needs while neglecting their own. This relentless giving is not a true act of kindness but a plea for recognition and love that they believe they can only earn by serving others. Over time, their self-sacrifice becomes a draining force, as they give and give until there's nothing left, all the while hoping that someone will finally notice them, appreciate them, and validate their existence. Yet, no matter how much they do, it never seems to be enough, leaving them feeling empty and unfulfilled.

The Emotional Parasites: Feeding on your Energy, these Vampires latch onto you with a grip that never loosens, drawing emotional sustenance from your kindness and support. They thrive on your energy, using your empathy as a lifeline to keep their own emotional chaos at bay. But as they feed on your goodwill, they leave you feeling drained, depleted, and burdened by their relentless demands. Being around them feels like you're being siphoned of your vitality, as if their emotional needs are slowly draining the life force from your very soul.

Breaking the Curse of the Needy One

To escape the clutches of The Needy One, you must craft a circle of protection around your energy, setting firm boundaries that even the darkest shadow cannot cross. While it's noble to offer support, it's not your duty to be their endless source of validation or reassurance. Encourage them to seek out their own inner strength, to discover self-sufficiency within themselves rather than relying on others to fill their emotional void. At times, you may need to step back, allowing them to navigate their own chilly corridors, even if it means must face their own fears alone. Remember, your energy is sacred. Guard it well, and don't let The Needy One drain it away into the shadows.

12TH LAIR

Energy Vampire in the Love Lane

Ah, Love Lane—a place where hearts intertwine under the glow of a moonlit sky, where whispers of sweet nothings drift like the gentle rustle of autumn leaves. But beware, dear traveler, for even the most enchanting of love stories can take a dark, twisted turn.

Just as the full moon casts eerie shadows on a quiet night, love too can be overshadowed by lurking presences—Energy Vampires dressed as lovers, draining the very essence of your soul—welcome to the enchanted halls of relationships, where the chill of these sinister beings can turn what should be a romantic tale into a chilling horror story.

Let's explore how the first 11 Energy Vampires sabotage love.

Soul Suckers: The Narcissists

In the uncertain halls of relationships, the Soul Suckers are the true masters of manipulation, the narcissists who charm their way into your life only to drain your emotional well-being dry. These sinister partners craft their own spotlight, ensuring every moment revolves around their desires and needs. In the beginning, they shower you with attention, making you feel like the center of their universe, but it's all a cunning ruse.

As time goes on, their true nature emerges—they overshadow your achievements with their exaggerated tales, twist conversations to keep themselves at the center, and demand constant validation, offering nothing in return. The Soul Sucker's love is conditional, a mere tool to keep you tethered, feeding their ego while leaving you emotionally depleted. You're left feeling like you're trapped in a cursed carnival, where everything is an illusion designed to siphon your energy and erode your self-worth, until you're just a shadow of your former self.

Phantoms of Chaos: The Drama Queens

If your love life feels like a never-ending rollercoaster of drama and chaos, you might be entangled with a Phantom of Chaos, otherwise known as the Drama Queen. These Energy Vampires thrive on stirring up trouble, turning minor mishaps into full-blown horror shows. They feed on the emotional turmoil they create, ensuring that the spotlight never strays far from their own antics. Before you know it, you're caught in their whirlwind, with barely any time to think about your own needs or feelings.

Denial Demons: Twisters of Reality

In the eerie halls of love, Denial Demons twist reality to suit their narrative. They refuse to acknowledge their flaws, deflect blame, and manipulate the truth to keep you off-balance. In relationships, they craft an alternate reality where they're always right, and you're perpetually in the wrong. This gaslighting leaves you questioning your own perceptions, making you doubt your sanity as you try to make sense of the tangled web they weave.

Wailing Spirits: The Perpetual Victims

These Energy Vampires haunt the love lane with their endless tales of woe. They cast themselves as the eternal victims, drawing you into their web of pity and sorrow. Every slight, every inconvenience, is turned into a tragedy of epic proportions, with you playing the role of their savior. But no matter how much you console or support them, their wails never cease. Their goal is to keep you focused on their needs, draining you of energy and leaving you feeling helpless and burdened.

Cauldron Crawlers: The Clingy Critters

In love and relationships, these are the ones who refuse to let you rise. They fear change, terrified of losing you to a world beyond their dark, familiar waters. Every time you try to grow or seek new opportunities, they pull you back into the murky depths, anchoring you with their insecurities. These Energy Vampires are not malevolent, but their fears become chains that bind you to the bottom of the cauldron, preventing you from reaching the surface where the light of growth and progress awaits.

Gloom Mongers: Harbingers of Despair

These are the vampires who cast a shadow over love, turning what should be joyous moments into somber affairs. They thrive on negativity, always focusing on the dark side of life. In a relationship, they drain your energy with their constant complaints and pessimism, making it difficult to see the light. They pull you into their pit of despair, where every day feels like a spooky rerun of the same grim tale. With a Gloom Monger by your side, it's hard to find happiness, as their gloom overshadows every bright moment.

Shadow Controller: Master of Manipulation

This is the vampire who seeks to dominate your every move, turning love into a game of control. They dictate how you should act, what you should think, and even how you should feel. Their manipulation is subtle, often disguised as concern or advice, but it's true purpose is to bind you to their will. Under the Shadow Controller's gaze, you become a mere puppet, your strings pulled by their invisible hand. This vampire thrives on your submission, feeding off the power they hold over you.

Chronic Critics: The Unrelenting Judges

Being with a Chronic Critic feels like you're under constant scrutiny, where nothing you do is ever good enough. In love, this vampire constantly points out your flaws, making you feel like you can never measure up. Their criticism is relentless, eroding your self-esteem and leaving you doubting your worth. The Chronic Critic's goal is to keep you small, trapped in a cycle of self-doubt, where their voice is the only one you hear. With every cutting remark, they chip away at your confidence, turning what should be a partnership into a one-sided judgment.

Deceptive Gaslighters: Twisters of Truth

In the twisted world of Love, these are the master of psychological manipulation, twisting your sense of reality until you no longer trust your own perceptions. They deny things they've said or done, rewrite history, and make you question your sanity. In love, this Energy Vampire turns every conversation into a mind game, leaving you feeling lost and disoriented. The Gaslighter's goal is to keep you dependent on them, trapped in a troubled maze where they hold the only key to what's real and what's not.

Toxic Gossips: Purveyors of Discord

Trust becomes a fragile thing when secrets are twisted into weapons, and rumors spread like wildfire. The Toxic Gossip thrives on spreading rumors and secrets, stirring up drama and discord in your relationship. They revel in the chaos they create, using your secrets as weapons to control you. In love, they turn trust into a fragile thing, easily shattered by their poisonous words. The Toxic Gossip's goal is to keep you off-balance, always wondering who you can trust, as they weave their web of lies and half-truths around you.

Needy Ones: The Emotional Vampires

These vampires cling to you like a shadow, constantly seeking validation and reassurance. In love, their endless demands drain your emotional reserves, leaving you feeling exhausted and overwhelmed. They expect you to be their emotional anchor, their source of strength, and their guiding light, but they offer little in return. Over time, their neediness becomes a weight too heavy to bear, pulling you down into the depths of emotional fatigue.

Unshackling Toxic Love

Relationships entrapped by Energy Vampires are like being caught in an endless horror movie—always running, always afraid, never at peace. But you have the power to rewrite the script. Love shouldn't be a curse, draining your energy and trapping you into a nightmare. It should be a partnership where both people thrive, share joy, and grow together.

If you're trapped in the web of a toxic love, it's time to summon your inner Halloween Wizard, grab your Energy Vampire Blaster, and unleash a storm of courage, strength, and faith to banish those fiendish forces for good. Picture yourself wielding a powerful talisman, crackling with energy, ready to send those shadowy vampires fleeing back into the darkness. No more hiding in the shadows, no more letting them drain your essence—this is your moment to rise as the ultimate Blaster, reclaiming your power, your freedom, and your life.

Step 1: Arm Yourself with Courage

Courage is the fiery blast that lights up the darkness and gives you the resolve to face the sinister truths that have been lurking in the shadows. To summon your courage:

Unmask the Horror: Shine a light on the chilling reality of your situation. Acknowledge that the relationship is a cursed bond that no longer serves you and remind yourself that you deserve so much more.

Declare Your Worth: Stand before the mirror, gaze into your own eyes, and chant, "I am worthy of love, respect, and happiness. No ghoul can take that from me."

Envision Your Escape: Close your eyes and see yourself breaking free from the haunted house of your past. Picture the lightness in your step as you leave the shadows behind, moving toward a brighter, ghost-free future.

Step 2: Strengthen Your Spirit

Strength is your shield, protecting you from the dark forces that seek to pull you back into their clutches. To fortify your spirit:

Rally Your Coven: Gather your trusted allies—friends, family, or a wise sage—who can offer you the strength and guidance you need. Together, you'll form a circle of protection, warding off the darkness.

Draw Your Boundaries: With a steady hand, carve a line in the sand. Let the spirits know what is no longer acceptable in your life. These boundaries are your protective wards, keeping the dark forces at bay.

Brew Your Potions of Self-Care: Engage in rituals that recharge your energy—whether it's a moonlit walk, a calming meditation, or indulging in hobbies that bring you joy. The more you nurture your spirit, the stronger your defenses become.

Step 3: Ignite Your Faith

Faith is the enchanted flame that guides you through the misty unknown, illuminating the path to freedom. To kindle your faith:

Trust in the Magic: Believe that every step you take away from the cursed relationship is a step toward your true destiny. Know that while the journey may be fraught with challenges, it will ultimately lead to your salvation.

Embrace the Mystery: The future may be shrouded in fog, but have faith that the unknown holds new, wondrous possibilities. Trust that you have the power to shape your fate, no matter how dark the night.

Connect with Your Higher Power: Whether through ancient rituals, meditation, or quiet reflection, strengthen your connection to something greater than yourself. Let this higher power be your guiding star, leading you out of the darkness.

Step 4: Take Decisive Action

Action is where your courage, strength, and faith come together in a blazing inferno, burning away the chains that have held you captive. To take action:

Craft Your Escape Spell: Whether it's finding a new lair, securing your financial independence, or seeking wise counsel, map out the steps you need to break free from the cursed relationship.

Cast Your Spell with Determination: Once your escape spell is complete, execute it with unwavering resolve. Set the date, gather your supplies, and make your move—leap through the window as the first rays of dawn chase away the night.

Embrace Your New Dawn: As you step away from the cursed bond, celebrate your triumph. Embrace the new chapter of your life with open arms, knowing that you have reclaimed your power and your freedom.

With each step, you're not just escaping the shadows—you're banishing them with the full force of your will and magical might. Your courage, strength, and faith are the enchanted tools that will carry you to safety and beyond, into a life filled with light, love, and endless possibilities. So, take a deep breath, steady your aim, and unleash your Energy Vampire Blaster with everything you have got. The dawn is breaking, and it's time to step into the light, free from the grip of the darkness that once held you captive.

13TH LAIR

Haunted Hearts

Ah, the shadows of loneliness, anxiety, and stress—they sneak through the corners of our minds like lurking phantoms, waiting to pounce when we least expect it. When these ghoulish feelings rear their eerie heads, many of us fall into the trap of reaching for those quick fixes, those emotional bandages that seem to soothe our spirits but leave our wounds festering beneath the surface.

These little habits may appear harmless, even comforting, but beware—they're as deceptive as a half-spoken whisper, offering false refuge while leading you deeper into the encrypted halls of your own mind. Let's shine a ghostly light on these sneaky bandages, revealing their true nature before they ensnare you in their sinister spell.

The Comfort Food Consumer: Feasting with the Hungry Goblins

Picture this: After a long day of battling life's monsters, you find yourself cozying up on the couch with a cauldron-sized tub of ice cream. The first bite feels like a sweet spell, soothing your frazzled nerves. But beware! This isn't just about enjoying a treat; it's about using food as a magical charm to ward off those pesky emotions. The Comfort Food Consumer feeds their emotional hunger with snacks and sweets, only to feel weighed down by the ghostly aftereffects—both physically and emotionally. The relief is fleeting, like a ghost vanishing at dawn, leaving behind a trail of regret.

The Retail Therapy Addict: Shopping with Shadows

Ah, the allure of the shopping spree, where every click and purchase feel like casting a charm to banish your blues. But beware, dear soul, for this is the trickiest of Energy Vampire Band-Aids. The Retail Therapy Addict finds momentary joy in something shiny and new, but this joy is as fleeting as a wisp of smoke. As the thrill fades, it's often replaced by haunting pains of guilt or the dread of an empty bank account. Like a cursed object from a dark magicians shop, the more you accumulate, the heavier the burden becomes.

The Social Media Scroller: Trapped in the Digital Web

The Social Media Scroller is a creature of habit, always seeking validation through 'likes' and comments. It's as if they're trapped in a digital web, spinning through the endless feed in search of approval. But what they find is a comparison trap, where their life never quite measures up to the curated perfection of others. They're seduced by the emotional residue of inadequacy, believing they'll never be as good as the influencers they follow. The screen becomes a mirror that reflects their insecurities back at them, distorting their self-worth like a funhouse mirror at a creepy carnival.

The News Junkie: Ensnared by the Ever-Twisting Headlines

For the News Junkie, the constant stream of headlines is like a cursed crystal ball, always revealing the latest calamities and political turmoil. They're drawn to it, seeking a sense of control over the chaotic world, but this control is merely an illusion—a dark enchantment that holds them captive. Each scroll and click feeds their anxiety, like a relentless vampire draining their inner calm. Trapped in an endless loop of doom-scrolling, they become addicted to the negativity, unable to break free from the dark energy that saps their peace of mind.

The Serial Dater: Haunted by Loneliness

The Serial Dater is captivated by the fear of being alone, so they jump from one relationship to the next, hoping to fill the void within. Each new partner is like a bandage slapped over a wound that needs time and care to heal. But the mirrors of past relationships linger, whispering doubts and insecurities into their ear. Instead of finding love, they end up traumatized by the same old fears, carrying their baggage from one relationship to another, never giving themselves a chance to rest and recover.

The Jack-of-All-Triggers: Master of Distractions

This restless soul is always on the lookout for the next distraction—a binge-worthy series, an impulsive shopping spree, anything to avoid facing the shadows lurking within. The Jack-of-All-Triggers jumps from one activity to the next, trying to escape their feelings of emptiness and inadequacy. But like a ghost chained to its past, they can never quite break free. These distractions are like cobwebs in an old attic—easy to get caught in, but they do nothing to clear out the dust and darkness.

Unmasking the Energy Vampire Bandages

These Energy Vampire bandages might offer a quick fix, but they're like trying to hold back the tide with a broomstick. They give you temporary relief, but they don't tackle the deeper, darker emotions lurking in the shadows. Whether it's comfort food, retail therapy, endless scrolling, news obsession, serial dating, or constant distractions, these habits only serve to cover up the cracks in your emotional foundation. The trick is to recognize these bandages for what they are—temporary patches over a deeper wound—and to seek out more genuine ways to heal.

Banishing the Emptiness

To truly banish these Energy Vampire Band-Aids, you need to summon the courage to face your Energy Vampires head-on. Start by acknowledging your feelings—whether it's loneliness, anxiety, or sadness—without reaching for a quick fix. Seek out healthier coping mechanisms that nourish your soul rather than drain it. It might be time to practice some self-care rituals, seek support from friends or a counselor, or dive into activities that bring genuine joy and fulfillment.

Remember, true healing doesn't come from covering up the wound but from tending to it with care. So, step away from the temptations of these Band-Aids and embrace the journey of self-discovery and growth. It's time to reclaim your power and banish those emotional vampires for good.

PART II

Unmasking your Inner Energy Vampire

Beware, brave Blaster, for the most devious of all Energy Vampires is the one that lurks within—the Inner Vampire. This sneaky creature feeds off your doubts, insecurities, and negative self-talk, draining your energy from the inside out. It's a master of disguise, often whispering in your own voice, convincing you that you're not good enough or that your dreams are out of reach. But as a true Energy Vampire Blaster, you have the power to turn the tables and blast this inner menace into oblivion! In this part, you'll learn the powerful techniques to expose, confront, and defeat your Inner Vampire, reclaiming your inner light and transforming that lurking darkness into unstoppable confidence and strength.

Your Inner Vampire

Always watching you.
Following you everywhere you go.

Shall we uncover the mysteries of the Inner Vampire?

Picture this sinister force, if you dare—a Chronic Critic lurking in the darkest corners of your mind, feeding on your insecurities and whispering venomous doubts into your ear. This shadowy creature thrives on your fears, constantly reminding you of every past mistake, making you question your worth, and keeping you in the eerie shadows of your own potential.

But where does this ghastly presence come from; you wonder? It's a potion brewed from the darkest ingredients of your past—a dash of a critical parent's biting words, a pinch of the cruel taunts from childhood bullies, a spoonful of harsh lessons from a teacher's cold gaze, and a cauldron bubbling over with society's impossible standards. Stir in a sprinkle of comparison to others and a lingering fear of failure, and you have summoned the Inner Vampire into your life. These experiences plant seeds of doubt that grow into your own personal tormentor, painting your world with a sinister shade of despair.

Imagine this: within the shadowy corridors of your mind, there exists a phantom—an ominous figure that delights in highlighting your every flaw and mistake. It revels in your insecurities, constantly whispering, "You're not good enough," "You'll just stumble again," or "Who could ever love someone like you?" This is your Inner Vampire—the embodiment of toxic thoughts, self-doubt, and the haunting fears that chain you to your past.

But how does this pesky critter worm its way into your head? It doesn't just appear overnight—no, its presence is far more insidious. Born from the twisted echoes of past experiences—like the cutting words of a critical parent, the deep scars left by heartbreak, or the relentless pressure of society's unattainable ideals—this Inner Vampire slowly creeps into your consciousness, whispering its dark incantations into your ear.

This vampire of self-doubt keeps you tethered to toxic beliefs, constantly haunting you with thoughts like, "Is this really all I deserve?" or "Am I even worthy of something better?" It's as if you're rolling out the red carpet for these dark forces, inviting them to make a home in your mind and cloud your judgment.

Our Inner Vampire loves to feast on your insecurities, convincing you that you're not meant for love, respect, or happiness. It whispers that staying in a rotten relationship is safer than daring to break free and start anew. It's as if you're trapped in a haunted house of your own making, too frightened to step into the light and reclaim your life.

But here is the trick—the true magic lies within you, for you hold more power over these shadowy figures than you have been led to believe. It all begins with calling their bluff, challenging the dark tales they spin, and reclaiming the light that's rightfully yours.

Which of These Inner Vampire Vibes Are Haunting You?

The Perfectionist Predator

This shadowy figure haunts the corners of your achievements, always ready to strike with a venomous hiss. This creature points out every tiny flaw, no matter how small. Finished a project? It whispers, "It could have been better." Reached a goal? It sneers, "But did you see how much better everyone else is doing?" This vampire sets impossibly high standards, ensuring you always fall short in its cold, unblinking eyes, fueling a never-ending cycle of self-doubt and dissatisfaction. The real terror lies in the belief that perfection is the key to being liked and accepted—a belief born from not accepting yourself as you truly are.

The Fear Feaster

A vampire that thrives on your deepest anxieties. This menace loves to feast on every "what if" scenario you can conjure up in the dead of night. Planning to ask for a raise? "What if you get rejected?" it whispers, its breath icy against your ear. Thinking about starting something new? "Remember how the last one ended," it reminds you, its voice a chilling echo of past heartbreaks. This vampire keeps you locked in a state of inaction, paralyzed by the fear of what might go wrong, feeding on your apprehension like a ravenous beast.

The Regret Reaper

Lurking in the graveyard of your past mistakes is—a ghastly figure that digs up your buried failures, no matter how deeply you have tried to forget them. This tormentor won't let you forget that embarrassing thing you said five years ago or that opportunity you missed because you hesitated. "You always mess up," it taunts, keeping you shackled to your past and doubting your ability to make better decisions in the future. **The Regret Reaper** thrives on your misery, keeping you chained to what once was, preventing you from stepping into what could be.

The Validation Vampire

A cunning creature that feeds on your need for approval and acceptance. This vampire convinces you that your worth is determined solely by what others think of you. "Did they like your presentation, or were they just being polite?" it questions, its fangs gleaming as it prepares to drain your self-worth. "If you don't attend that event, everyone will think less of you," it warns, keeping you in a constant state of anxiety over potentially disappointing others. The **Validation Vampire** drives you to exhaust yourself in the pursuit of pleasing everyone, leaving little room for self-care or understanding your own needs and desires.

But take heart! The vampire begins to wither as you recognize your intrinsic value, independent of external validation. Learning to love and accept yourself, flaws and all, is like holding up a cross to this vampire. As you establish boundaries, prioritize self-care, and embrace your authentic self, you begin to starve this vampire of its power. Slowly but surely, its voice becomes a distant whisper, overshadowed by your own inner strength and self-assurance.

The Phantom of "Never Enough"

There's another phantom that haunts the halls of your mind—the Inner Vampire of Scarcity. This elusive specter whispers in the dead of night, convincing you that there's never enough—never enough time, never enough money, never enough love, never enough of *anything*. It thrives in the shadows of your thoughts, making you believe that abundance is an illusion and that you must cling to what little you have for fear of losing it all.

This Scarcity Phantom loves to parade through the corridors of your mind, casting spells of doubt and fear. It tells you that you must hoard your resources, guard your heart, and be wary of every opportunity because there's not enough to go around. It keeps you trapped in a mindset of lack, where every decision is weighed down by the fear of scarcity, and every choice feels like a risk too great to take.

Picture it: the Scarcity Phantom hovering over you as you consider a new opportunity, whispering in your ear, "What if this doesn't work out? What if you lose everything? What if there's nothing left for you?" This ghostly figure thrives on your hesitation, feeding on the fear that there's never enough to go around, and that you must settle for less to avoid losing it all.

But here is the twist in the tale—the Scarcity Phantom is nothing more than an illusion, a trick of the mind conjured by past experiences and societal pressures. It's a phantom that can be banished with a simple shift in perspective. The moment you recognize that abundance is all around you, that opportunities are plentiful, and that you are deserving of all the good things life has to offer, the Scarcity Phantom begins to fade into the shadows.

To defeat this phantom, you must summon the power of belief—the belief that you are worthy, that there is enough, and that abundance is your birthright. With each step you take toward embracing this mindset, the Scarcity Phantom loses its grip on you, its whispers turning to echoes that fade into the distance.

So, as you continue on your journey to becoming a Halloween Energy Vampire Blaster, remember to keep an eye out for the Scarcity Phantom. When it rears its ghostly head, remind yourself that abundance is not a myth but a reality that you can tap into at any time. Cast away the fear of lack, embrace the belief in plenty, and watch as the Scarcity Phantom shrinks into the shadows, unable to haunt you any longer.

These **Inner Vampires** are masters of stealth, creeping up on you when the shadows are longest, undermining your confidence with whispers as cold as a ghostly breeze, and nibbling away at your happiness like unseen ghouls in the night. But here is the twist—spotting these saboteurs is like shining a lantern in a dark, cobwebbed room. The moment that eerie light touches them, their power starts to wane, and they're no longer the invisible terrors they once were.

Once you have locked eyes with these fiends, it's time to go on the offensive. When they hiss, "You're not good enough," hit back with, "Says who?" Challenge them like you would any phantom in the night, and demand proof. Spoiler alert: they won't have any, because like all shadows, they're nothing but smoke and mirrors.

Here's an essential spell: Be kind to yourself. This battle isn't about scolding yourself for having listened to them in the first place. It's about realizing you're human, and these doubts are as natural as shadows at twilight, but far less useful.

As you sharpen your skills—questioning the authenticity of their whispers, unearthing the real truths buried beneath their lies, and practicing a bit of self-love—something magical begins to happen. Those once-menacing vampires start to shrink. They transform from monsters into mere echoes, like the rustling of leaves in an otherworldly forest or the distant wail of a ghostly wind. Eventually, they're just part of the eerie scenery of your mind, noticeable but no longer capable of derailing your path.

Dream Weavers and Dream Stealers

Architects of Your Inner Vampire

In the shadowy corridors of life, where whispers of the past echo through the walls, our self-worth, habits, and perceptions are often shaped by two powerful forces: Dream Weavers and Dream Stealers. These figures, much like spirits from another realm, haunt our past and present, crafting the narrative we tell ourselves—whether it's one of empowerment and possibility or one of fear and limitation. Understanding their influence is the key to breaking free from these chains and reclaiming control over our destiny.

Dream Weavers: The Enchanters of Self-Worth

Dream Weavers are the benevolent wizards of the heart, those emotionally and intellectually healthy parents, teachers, mentors, and role models who know how to weave confidence, love, and significance into the very fabric of our being. They understand that self-confidence is a rare and perishable flower, needing constant nurturing under the moon's gentle glow. With every word of encouragement, every challenge to think critically, and every lesson on resilience, they strengthen the belief in our own worth and potential.

Dream Weavers possess a mystical perspective, teaching that failure is not a dead-end but a stepping stone to greater achievements. They understand that life's setbacks are merely temporary defeats, opportunities to learn and grow stronger. When we stumble, they offer a guiding hand, encouraging us to rise again, to see failure not as a reflection of our worth but as feedback on our journey to success.

These magical figures focus on what we do right rather than our shortcomings. They demonstrate the power of self-reliance, emotional consistency, and mental strength, leading by example and building trust. By doing so, they help us forge a resilient, positive self-image. Children of Dream Weavers grow into confident, optimistic adults who believe in possibilities and approach life with a sense of adventure and hope.

Dream Stealers: The Creators of Inner Vampires

But lurking in the shadows are the Dream Stealers, sinister counterparts to the Dream Weavers. These figures, often parents or influential adults, are the ones who unknowingly—or sometimes knowingly—

plant the seeds of the Inner Vampire within us. Their harsh words, neglect, and fear-based teachings become the bricks in the walls of our self-doubt and insecurity.

Dream Stealers raise their children through fear, anger, and control. They may not understand the dark magic they're wielding, but their actions imprint deeply on young minds. Children absorb their negativity like a sponge, internalizing beliefs that they are not good enough, smart enough, or deserving of love. These toxic beliefs then grow into the Inner Vampire, a shadowy figure that whispers fear and self-doubt into our ears long into adulthood.

Children raised by Dream Stealers often find themselves in a twilight zone of inner conflict. They crave love and approval from those who should be their protectors and guides, yet they are simultaneously harmed by these very figures. The result is an emotional battlefield where the seeds of the Inner Vampire take root, growing stronger with each fear-based lesson learned.

The Dream Stealers' influence extends beyond the home. Teachers, religious leaders, and even friends can become Dream Stealers, embedding fear and doubt into our minds. Their warnings and criticisms become the lens through which we view the world, and over time, we start to believe that our dreams are unattainable, that we are unworthy, and that life is a series of obstacles rather than opportunities.

The Legacy of Dream Weavers and Dream Stealers

The legacy left by Dream Weavers and Dream Stealers is as profound as it is enduring. Dream Weavers craft a tapestry of hope, strength, and self-belief, empowering us to chase our dreams with confidence, much like a lantern guiding us through a dark forest. In contrast, Dream Stealers leave behind a haunted house of doubts, fears, and insecurities, trapping us in a cycle of self-sabotage and limiting beliefs, with the shadows of their influence lurking in every corner.

Those raised by Dream Weavers find themselves equipped with the enchanted tools needed to navigate life's challenges with resilience and optimism. Setbacks are seen as mere temporary haunts, and we pursue our dreams with an unwavering determination. On the other hand, those raised by Dream Stealers may struggle with a pervasive sense of inadequacy, their lives overshadowed by the Inner Vampire's whispering doubts, much like ghosts that refuse to rest.

But take heart, for the story doesn't end in darkness. Recognizing the influence of Dream Weavers and Dream Stealers is the first step in reclaiming our narrative. By acknowledging the impact these figures have had on our lives, we can begin the process of exorcising the past, rewriting our story, and silencing the Inner Vampire. Whether our past was shaped by Dream Weavers or Dream Stealers, the power to conjure a brighter future lies within us.

We have the choice to embrace the lessons of the Dream Weavers, focusing on our strengths and cultivating a mindset of growth and possibility. We can also confront and banish the fears planted by the Dream Stealers, freeing ourselves from their lingering shadows. In doing so, we transform our Inner Vampire from a force of sabotage into one of empowerment, guiding us toward a life filled with light, purpose, and fulfillment.

In this journey of self-discovery and transformation, we become our own Dream Weavers, crafting a new narrative of hope, strength, and limitless potential. The past may have shaped us, but it does not define us. The future is ours to create, and with the wisdom of the Dream Weavers and the courage to face our Inner Vampires, we can weave a life of joy, success, and boundless possibility.

Whispers from Your Inner Vampire

Beware when emotions like shame, guilt, anxiety, and fear creep up on you unexpectedly, lingering like uninvited ghosts at a unearthly gathering. These emotions often strike when you're vulnerable, casting a shadow over your mood and sapping your energy without a clear reason. You might find yourself spiraling into negative thinking, fixating on past mistakes, or worrying excessively about the future. These emotions can make you feel like you're stuck in a dark, endless tunnel with no escape. You may also notice a pattern of overthinking, self-criticism, and feeling emotionally drained after interacting with certain people or situations.

Emotions: The Haunting Signals of Your Inner World

Red Flags: Your emotions flicker like the lights in a haunted house, casting eerie shadows that signal something isn't quite right. When you find yourself repeatedly feeling down, anxious, or overwhelmed without a clear cause, it's a sure sign that your Inner Vampire is stirring from its slumber.

Are you being spooked by a particular emotion—fear, guilt, shame, or dread? These feelings might be stirred by memories long buried, trapping you in a ghostly loop of negativity. You might also notice physical manifestations of these emotions, like tension headaches or the weight of a phantom's hand pressing on your chest, reminding you that all is not well in your tainted heart.

The Power of Focus: Where Your Mind's Spotlight Shines

Red Flags: Your focus becomes a cursed spotlight, illuminating only the darkest corners of your mind, casting long, twisted shadows where your fears take shape. If you find yourself dwelling on worst-case scenarios, obsessing over the grim outcomes, or fixating on your deepest fears, it's clear that your Inner Vampire has taken control of the show.

You might notice that you're constantly anticipating disaster or expecting things to go wrong, as if a storm is always brewing on the horizon. Your thoughts drift like restless spirits, hovering over worries and what-ifs, making it nearly impossible to focus on anything bright or hopeful. This unholy focus can wrap you in a cloak of dread, a shadow that looms even during moments meant to be filled with joy.

Fear and Growth: The Two-Headed Monster

Red Flags: Fear is no longer just a shadowy figure—it's become a two-headed monster, feeding your Inner Vampire and blocking your path to growth. When fear stops you from pursuing opportunities or trying new things, it's a sign that it's taken control.

If you find yourself avoiding challenges or shying away from situations that could lead to personal growth, fear has become a barrier rather than a motivator. You might experience feelings of paralysis, where even small risks seem too daunting to take. This fear often disguises itself as practicality or caution, convincing you that staying in your comfort zone is the safest option.

Flipping the Script on Negative Emotions

Red Flags: Negative emotions have taken center stage, casting a gloomy spell over your thoughts. If you're constantly replaying past mistakes or dwelling on your flaws, your Inner Vampire is directing the show.

You might catch yourself in a cycle of self-blame, where every thought leads back to something you did wrong. These emotions may lead you to avoid certain situations or people out of fear of judgment. Over time, this can erode your self-esteem and make it difficult to see the positives in your life.

Embracing Your Inner Ghouls

Red Flags: You have been running from your emotions like they're ghouls in a haunted house, but now they're catching up to you. If you have been avoiding your feelings or trying to suppress them, they'll only grow stronger.

You might notice that your emotions are becoming harder to ignore, showing up in unexpected ways—like sudden outbursts or overwhelming feelings of sadness or anger. These emotions often intensify when you're stressed or tired, making it even more difficult to keep them at bay. You may also find that you're turning to unhealthy coping mechanisms, like overworking, overeating, or isolating yourself, to avoid dealing with your feelings.

Turning Fright into Might

Red Flags: Fear has morphed from a helpful guide into a paralyzing force, preventing you from taking action. If you have stopped moving forward because you're too afraid of what might happen, it's time to confront your Inner Vampire.

You might feel stuck in a state of inaction, where even the smallest decisions seem overwhelming. This fear often manifests as procrastination, indecision, or a constant need for reassurance. You may find yourself frequently asking, "What if it all goes wrong?" rather than focusing on the potential for success. This mindset can leave you feeling powerless, as though you're trapped in a never-ending cycle of doubt and hesitation.

The Isolated Tower of Perfectionism

Red Flags: The Isolated Tower of Perfectionism looms tall, casting a shadow over your every move. If you're constantly striving for unattainable standards and berating yourself for not meeting them, you're trapped in this grim fortress.

Inside this tower, you may find yourself obsessing over details, unable to finish projects because they're never "perfect" enough. The fear of failure haunts you, making it difficult to take risks or try new things. You might also notice that you're overly critical of yourself, focusing on what you did wrong rather than celebrating your successes. This perfectionism can lead to burnout, as you push yourself beyond your limits in an effort to achieve the impossible.

The Echoing Caves of Isolation

Red Flags: The Echoing Caves of Isolation are closing in, amplifying your self-doubt and leaving you feeling disconnected. If you have withdrawn from others or feel like you're facing life's challenges alone, these caverns are keeping you captive.

You might feel an overwhelming sense of loneliness, even when you're surrounded by people. These feelings of isolation can lead to a lack of motivation, as you struggle to find the energy to engage with the world around you. You may also notice that you're avoiding social situations or turning down opportunities to connect with others. Over time, this isolation can create a vicious cycle, where the more you withdraw, the harder it becomes to reach out.

The Swamps of Stagnation

Red Flags: The Swamps of Stagnation are dragging you down, making every step forward feel like a struggle. If you have lost your motivation and feel stuck in a rut, you're sinking deeper into this murky mire.

You might find yourself repeating the same routines day after day, with no sense of progress or excitement. This stagnation can lead to feelings of boredom, frustration, and even hopelessness. You may notice that you're avoiding challenges or opportunities for growth, opting instead to stay in your comfort zone. Over time, this stagnation can drain your energy and leave you feeling disconnected from your goals and passions.

The Fortress of Victimhood

Red Flags: The Fortress of Victimhood has raised its walls, trapping you in a cycle of self-pity and helplessness. If you feel powerless to change your circumstances and blame external factors for your struggles, you're a prisoner in this fortress.

You might find yourself frequently complaining about your life, feeling like everything is out of your control. This victim mentality can lead to feelings of resentment, as you perceive the world as unfair and unforgiving. You may also notice that you're quick to blame others for your problems, rather than taking responsibility for your actions. Over time, this mindset can prevent you from taking the steps needed to improve your situation, leaving you feeling stuck and defeated.

The Quagmire of Blame

Red Flags: The Quagmire of Blame is pulling you under, trapping you in a cycle of fault-finding and evasion. If you're constantly pointing fingers and avoiding accountability, you're sinking deeper into this sticky pit.

You might find that you're quick to criticize others and slow to acknowledge your own mistakes. This blame-shifting behavior can create tension in your relationships, as others grow tired of being held responsible for your problems. You may also notice that you're defensive when confronted with feedback, making it difficult to learn and grow. Over time, this quagmire can erode trust and communication, leaving you feeling isolated and misunderstood.

The Sorcery of Questions

The Inner Vampire's secret weapon is the spell you cast upon yourself with questions. But beware—ask the wrong ones, and you might find yourself trapped in a dark, self-fulfilling prophecy.

Imagine this: you're in the dim corridors of your mind, and the questions you toss around act as incantations. If you ask, "Why do I always mess things up?" or "What's wrong with me?" you're essentially casting a spell that invites doubt and negativity into your life, allowing the Inner Vampire to grow stronger. It's like leaving the door to your mind wide open, inviting these dark forces to feast on your insecurities and fears.

These Inner Vampires thrive on disempowering questions. Consider questions like, "Why can't I ever get things right?" or "Why do bad things always happen to me?" These are the kinds of questions that keep you stuck in a relentless loop, endlessly replaying scenes of self-doubt and defeat. It's like you're casting spells that keep you trapped in a shadowy maze, where every turn leads to more confusion and despair.

Other sinister questions might include, "Why do people always take advantage of me?" or "Why am I never good enough for anyone?" These questions wrap you in a fog of negativity, blurring your vision of what's truly possible. Or perhaps you have caught yourself asking, "Why do I always end up alone?" or "Why does nothing ever work out for me?"—each one another spell that deepens the shadows around you, making it harder to see the light at the end of the tunnel.

But here is the twist—what if you could flip the script? What if, instead of inviting these creatures in, you turned the tables on them? Ask yourself, "What can I learn from this?" or "How can I grow stronger from this experience?" These questions are like sacred symbols that repel the vampires, forcing them to retreat into the shadows. They're empowering incantations that help you reclaim your strength and clarity, illuminating your path with newfound purpose and resilience.

Imagine the difference between asking, "Why do I always attract the wrong people?" versus "What can I do to attract more positive and supportive relationships?" The former drags you deeper into a pit of despair, while the latter opens up a world of possibilities, guiding you toward better choices and outcomes. Or consider the difference between, "Why am I always the one who gets hurt?" and "How can I protect my heart while still being open to love?" One keeps you in the role of the eternal victim, while the other empowers you to take control of your emotional well-being.

Each question you ask, each spell you cast—can either fortify your defenses or weaken them. When you choose questions that empower you, that focus on your strengths and potential, you strip the Inner Vampires of their power. They start to shrink, losing their grip on your mind, becoming nothing more than whispers in the wind, easily dismissed and forgotten.

But where does this haunting presence come from? It's a potion brewed from past experiences—a dash of a critical parent, a pinch of a tough breakup, a spoonful of societal expectations, and maybe even a splash of betrayal by someone you trusted. These experiences shape the questions we ask ourselves, often leading us down a path where we unknowingly give power to our Inner Vampires.

Recognizing the eerie link between your self-questioning and the power of your Inner Vampires is the first step in reclaiming your magical essence. By consciously choosing to ask empowering questions like, "What spells can I cast to create the life I desire?" or "How can I turn this challenge into a potion for growth?" you're weaving enchantments that build you up rather than tear you down. These questions are your mystical tools, transforming the dark, haunting figures of your doubts and fears into mere wisps of shadow, fading into the night.

The secret lies in being mindful of the spells you're casting with your thoughts. When you feel yourself spiraling into the abyss with questions that conjure the worst, halt the incantation. Flip the spell. Ask yourself questions that light up your path, that focus on your strengths, and that empower you to rise. Remember, you're the master spellcaster in your own life, and the questions you choose to ask can either summon more darkness or usher in the dawn. The magic is in your hands—wield it wisely.

The Haunting of Negative Beliefs

As we venture into the haunted house of negative beliefs, it's time to arm yourself with the tools of an Energy Vampire Blaster, empowering you to clear out the shadows and reclaim your personal power.

In this Haunted House, the walls whisper your deepest insecurities, and every corner harbors a new shadow of doubt. You have been living in this creepy abode far too long—tiptoeing through the corridors of self-doubt, peeking around corners filled with fear, and staring into the cracked mirrors that reflect every insecurity back at you. But guess what? It's time to stop being the victim in your own horror story and start taking back control. So, grab your flashlight because we're going on a ghost hunt to clear out these spooky spaces once and for all.

Room 1: The Hall of "I'm Not Good Enough"

First up, we step into the grand hall of "I'm Not Good Enough," where the ghostly echoes of past failures and the whispers of long-departed critics still drift through the air like a cold, lingering fog. This eerie chamber is adorned with portraits of every time you have stumbled, each one meticulously framed in regret and hung with care by the hands of doubt. Remember that moment you didn't land the job? Or when you felt the sting of embarrassment in front of everyone? Those memories are immortalized here, replaying like a possessed record that never seems to stop.

But here is the sinister secret of this hall—it's all smoke and mirrors, an illusion crafted by the shadows of your past. Yes, you have made mistakes. Who hasn't danced with a ghost or two? But this room is a trap, designed to keep you fixated on your flaws while conveniently eclipsing your strengths. The only way to escape its grasp? Acknowledge the imperfections, learn from them, and then shut down that old, creaky projector that's been looping the same tired horror flick. Remember, you're the director of your own life, so why keep replaying the blooper reel when you can start scripting a tale of triumph?

Room 2: The Chamber of "I Don't Deserve Success"

Next, we cautiously step into the Chamber of "I Don't Deserve Success," where the walls are draped with ancient chains and rusted shackles, relics of the self-imposed limitations that have held you back from realizing your true potential. Every time you have whispered to yourself that you're not good enough, every time you have settled for the crumbs instead of the feast, it was this chamber whispering in your ear. The floor is strewn with the bones of long-forgotten dreams—those brilliant ideas and grand ambitions you buried alive, convinced you were unworthy of them.

But here is the eerie twist: This chamber has never been locked. The door wasn't even closed. You have been sitting here, bound to the wall by nothing more than your own fears and misconceptions. The belief that you don't deserve success is just that—a belief, not a fact. The shackles? They're mere illusions, crumbling to dust the moment you dare to challenge them. So why linger in this cold, dark dungeon when the path to freedom is wide open before you? It's time to rise, shake off the cobwebs, and breathe life back into those old dreams. The night is dark, but the dawn of your success is waiting just outside.

Room 3: The Gallery of "What Will People Think?"

Welcome to the Gallery of "What Will People Think?"—a twisted exhibit where every piece of art is a distorted reflection of other people's opinions and judgments. The gallery is a hall of mirrors, each portrait showcasing the faces of those whose approval you have desperately sought. There's the disapproving boss, the judgmental relative, the high school bully—all of them frozen in time, their eyes following your every move, waiting for the slightest slip so they can revel in your missteps.

This room is a maze of people-pleasing, where every turn you take is dictated by the fear of what others might think. You tiptoe through life, hiding your true self, adjusting your actions to avoid those cold, critical stares. But here is the chilling truth—most of those people? They're not even watching. They're too consumed by their own horror shows to notice yours. So why let their imagined opinions dictate your every move? Why let their judgments hang on your walls like cursed paintings?

The escape route from this gallery is simple: realize that their opinions are just that—fleeting thoughts with no real power over you. They don't define your worth, and they certainly don't control your life unless you hand them the brush. It's time to take those paintings down, roll them up, and banish them to the attic of forgotten fears. This is your gallery, your life, and you alone get to choose what's on display.

Room 4: The Crypt of "I'll Never Change"

Descending into the Crypt of "I'll Never Change," we are met with the cold, unyielding grip of old habits and patterns, each marked by a crumbling tombstone.

Here lies "Procrastination," "Self-Doubt," and "Fear of Failure," each buried under the weight of the solemn vow that "I'll never change."

This crypt is a place where personal growth comes to die, where the air is thick with the chill of resignation, and the walls echo with the whisper of despair. It's a dark, damp resting place, sealed off by the belief that who you are today is who you'll always be.

But here is the twist in this tale—the crypt is not as eternal as it seems. The belief that you'll never change is no more permanent than the dirt covering these graves. Like any good horror story, there's a way out. Change, though frightening, is as inevitable as the rising of the undead. Even the most deeply buried fears and habits can be unearthed, moved aside, and transformed.

The first step to breaking free? Believing that change is possible. The second? Start digging. With each shovelful of effort, you uncover new possibilities, resurrecting the parts of yourself that were buried under layers of doubt and fear.

The crypt of "I'll Never Change" doesn't have to be your final resting place. Instead, let it be the very ground where your revival begins. Just as the most haunting fears can become the spark for transformation, this dark, confining space is where you can face the limiting beliefs that have kept you entombed. By acknowledging these buried thoughts, you can start the process of exorcising them—clearing out the old to make way for new, empowering beliefs. Your journey out of the crypt starts with a simple step: recognizing that these beliefs are ghosts of the past, and that you hold the power to lay them to rest and rise anew.

Room 5: The Tower of "I'm All Alone"

Now we ascend to the Tower of "I'm All Alone," a tall, foreboding structure that looms over the landscape of your mind, casting long shadows that chill the heart. This tower is a place of isolation, where the stones are cold and unyielding, and the higher you climb, the more the world below seems to disappear into the mist.

Each step upward feels heavier than the last, weighed down by the belief that no one truly understands you, that your struggles are yours alone to bear. The wind howls through the cracks in the walls, carrying with it the voices of isolation and despair, whispering that you're destined to face life's challenges without a soul to lean on.

As you reach the top, the view is bleak—a desolate expanse where connection and companionship seem like distant memories, lost to the fog that surrounds this towering prison. The Tower of "I'm All Alone" is designed to keep you trapped, convincing you that reaching out for help is futile, that the bridges to others have long since crumbled away.

The walls are adorned with faded portraits of solitary figures, each one a reflection of your deepest fears—fear of rejection, fear of vulnerability, fear of being truly seen and still remaining unseen. It's a lonely place, where the only company you have is the echo of your own thoughts, spiraling in a never-ending loop of self-doubt and isolation.

But here is the secret that the Tower of "I'm All Alone" doesn't want you to know—it's not as impenetrable as it seems. The isolation it imposes is an illusion, a trick of the mind that thrives on your fears and insecurities. The tower's walls, though thick, can be breached. The doors, though heavy, can be opened. The key lies in realizing that you are not truly alone; it's the belief that you are that keeps you trapped. The moment you choose to reach out, to let others in, the tower begins to crumble. The howling wind quiets, the portraits fade, and the once-solid walls start to crack, allowing rays of light to pierce through the darkness.

The climb down from the tower isn't easy—it requires courage to break the cycle of isolation, to reach out and risk being vulnerable. But each step you take away from the tower is a step toward connection, toward a world where you are understood and supported.

The more you open yourself to others, the more the fog lifts, revealing a landscape filled with potential allies, friends, and companions who share your struggles and joys. The Tower of "I'm All Alone" may have been a place of solitude, but it was never meant to be your home. It's time to descend, to walk out of the shadows and into the light of connection and community.

Room 6: The Vault of "No One Loves Me"

Venture now into the chilling Vault of "No One Loves Me," where the echoes of loneliness bounce relentlessly off the cold, unforgiving stone walls. This room is a prison of reflection, lined with tall, ancient mirrors that seem to stretch endlessly, each one casting back an image of solitude that feeds the haunting belief that you are unlovable. The air here is thick with the ghostly whispers of rejection and past heartaches, creating a labyrinth of doubt and fear that twists and turns, leaving you feeling lost and abandoned.

In this vault, the mirrors are more than just glass—they are enchanted to magnify your insecurities, distorting the truth until it's nearly unrecognizable. The reflections they show you are not realities, but twisted versions of your own fears, shaped by old wounds and misconceptions. They whisper lies, convincing you that love is something distant, something unattainable, something meant for others but never for you. It's a place where the shadows of past rejections loom large, casting long, dark figures that seem impossible to escape.

But here is the secret buried within the vault's cold walls: these mirrors, though they seem powerful, are fragile. The reflections they offer are warped by the barriers you have built to protect your heart, but those barriers can be dismantled. The truth is that love is not absent; it's simply been hidden behind the walls of fear and doubt that you have constructed over time. The key to escaping this vault lies in recognizing your own worth and daring to open your heart once again, allowing love to flow in where it has long been blocked.

To break free, you must shatter these mirrors of doubt. They may seem like unbreakable fortresses, but they are no match for the force of self-acceptance and love. As you face each mirror, see it for what it is—a distortion, not a reality. Smash through the shards of past hurts, let the glass fall to the ground, and watch as the light of truth pours in, dispelling the darkness. When you step out of this vault, you rewrite the narrative of your life, transforming it from one of isolation to one of love and acceptance.

Room 7: The Dungeon of "I'm Not Smart Enough"

Descend now into the murky depths of the Dungeon of "I'm Not Smart Enough," a shadowy pit where the chains of self-doubt and insecurity anchor you to the cold, unforgiving floor. The walls of this dungeon are etched with haunting inscriptions, each one a reminder of moments when you felt inadequate or were cruelly told that you lacked the intelligence to succeed. These carvings dig deep, echoing with the voices of past failures and missed opportunities, creating an atmosphere thick with despair and self-judgment.

Yet, this dungeon is not as solid as it seems. Its very foundations are built on a crumbling bedrock of false beliefs and harsh comparisons. Intelligence is not a one-size-fits-all measurement; it's a rich, diverse spectrum that includes far more than mere academic prowess. It encompasses wisdom, creativity, emotional insight, and a host of other qualities that often go unrecognized in the narrow definitions imposed by others. The dungeon thrives on your acceptance of these limiting beliefs, keeping you shackled to a narrow view of what it means to be smart.

But here is the key to your escape: redefine what intelligence means to you. Recognize that it's not a fixed trait but a dynamic, ever-evolving force that you can nurture and grow. Equip yourself with the tools of learning—curiosity, persistence, and a willingness to embrace new challenges. As you feed your mind with knowledge and allow your unique strengths to shine, the chains of doubt that have held you down will begin to weaken, link by link.

With each step you take towards learning and growth, the dungeon loses its grip on you. The inscriptions that once tormented you fade into the background as new, empowering beliefs take their place. The doors of this shadowy prison, which once seemed impenetrable, start to creak open, allowing the light of understanding to flood in. And as you walk out of the Dungeon of "I'm Not Smart Enough," you leave behind the misconceptions that once confined you, stepping into a world where your intellect is recognized in all its multifaceted brilliance.

Room 8: The Corridor of "They're Better Than Me"

Enter the narrow, winding Corridor of "They're Better Than Me," where the walls are adorned with towering statues of peers, each one cast in the unforgiving stone of envy and comparison. These statues loom large, their achievements seemingly far grander than your own, casting long, oppressive shadows that make you feel small and insignificant. The air is thick with the weight of self-doubt, and every step you take feels sluggish, as if you're trudging through a mire of inadequacy. The corridor traps you in an endless loop of comparison, where each stride forward is met with the disheartening thought that someone else has already done it better, faster, or more successfully.

But here is the truth about this corridor—it's an illusion crafted by the mind, a trick of perspective that distorts the true nature of your journey. The statues, while impressive, are not meant to overshadow you; they are simply markers of different paths, each unique and shaped by its own challenges and triumphs. The escape from this stifling corridor doesn't lie in outpacing these statues or tearing them down—it lies in shifting your focus from them to yourself.

Your journey is yours alone, incomparable to any other. The achievements of others are not measures of your worth, but rather, they are inspirations, proof that success comes in many forms and is within your reach, too. To break free from this corridor, you must light your own torch—a symbol of your individuality and self-worth. Illuminate your own path by celebrating your achievements, no matter how small they may seem. Acknowledge the growth and progress you have made on your own terms, and let that light guide you forward.

As you walk down this corridor with your torch held high, the statues begin to fade into the background. Their once-intimidating presence is replaced by the warm glow of self-confidence and self-acceptance. The oppressive atmosphere lifts, and the corridor that once felt endless and suffocating opens up, revealing a path that is entirely yours to walk. With each step, you distance yourself from the shadows of comparison, embracing your unique journey and the unshakable truth of your individual worth.

Room 9: The Maze of "I Should Have Known Better"

Step into the twisting Maze of "I Should Have Known Better," where every winding path is a haunting reminder of decisions that went awry and opportunities that slipped through your fingers. The walls of this labyrinth are woven with thorny vines of regret, each thorn pricking at your conscience, whispering accusations of "You should have known better." The more you wander, the more the maze confuses and disorients, trapping you in a loop of self-recrimination, endlessly circling back to the missteps of your past.

But here is the key to escaping this thorny maze: Hindsight, while tempting to trust, is a trickster, showing you not the truth of the past, but a distorted vision of what might have been. The maze thrives on your guilt and regret, feeding off the belief that you should have predicted every outcome, foreseen every consequence. Yet, the reality is that we are all blind to the future, navigating life with the best knowledge we have at the moment.

To break free from the maze, you must embrace forgiveness—both for the person you were and the choices you made with the limited knowledge you had. With each act of self-forgiveness, the thorns retract, and the walls of the maze begin to dissolve, revealing a clearer path forward. As you forgive yourself, the maze that once ensnared you loses its power, and the echoes of "You should have known better" fade into silence.

With the maze behind you, you step into the present, no longer haunted by the ghosts of past decisions. Armed with the wisdom gained from your experiences, you can now make choices with confidence, free from the burden of regret. The path ahead is no longer a twisting maze but a straight road illuminated by the light of self-compassion and newfound clarity.

Room 10: The Observatory of "What If?"

Ascend to the towering heights of the Observatory of "What If?", a place where the stars of possibility shine in every direction, and the telescopes are aimed not at the heavens, but at the countless alternate realities of your life. Here, each telescope offers a glimpse into a different path you could have taken, a different choice you might have made. The visions are alluring scenes of "what could have been" that often appear far more glittering than the life you're living now. This observatory can be as enchanting as it is paralyzing, trapping you in a web of endless speculation, where the "what ifs" keep you from embracing the life you have.

But to escape this celestial trap, you must shift your focus. Instead of peering endlessly into the telescopes of past possibilities, turn your gaze to the windows that offer a clear view of the present reality. The observatory may be filled with seductive visions of what might have been, but the true beauty lies in the here and now. Each choice you have made, each path you have followed, has woven the intricate tapestry of your life, full of lessons learned and experiences gained.

To leave the Observatory of "What If?", you must let go of the regrets tied to the roads not taken and appreciate the unique journey you're on. Recognize that even those choices that seemed flawed at the time have contributed to your growth, resilience, and wisdom. Celebrate the present moment and the life you have crafted from the choices you did make. With this realization, you can step out of the observatory, leaving behind the shadowy allure of alternate realities, and walk confidently into the light of the present, where the true adventure of your life unfolds.

Room 11: The Catacombs of "I'm Just a Failure"

Venture into the shadowy depths of Room 11: The Catacombs of "I'm Just a Failure," where the air is thick with the musty scent of defeat and the walls are lined with relics of your past missteps. Every artifact—a botched project, a broken relationship, a missed opportunity—whispers tales of inadequacy, their voices echoing through the dimly lit corridors like the mournful wails of lost souls. In these eerie halls, the shadows of self-doubt stretch long, casting distorted reflections of your deepest fears and amplifying the illusion that you are trapped in a never-ending nightmare of failure.

But here is the secret hidden within these catacombs—a truth buried beneath the layers of illusion. Each so-called failure, looming like a phantom in the darkness, is not a final defeat but a lesson, a stepping stone on your journey toward growth and resilience. To escape these suffocating depths, ignite the Lanterns of Perspective to cut through the gloom, revealing that what appeared to be failures were actually invaluable experiences, each one shaping you into a stronger, wiser version of yourself.

As you navigate this maze, be sure to collect the Coins of Success tucked away in its shadowy corners, each one representing a victory, no matter how small. These coins are the reminders of your strength, your perseverance, and your ability to rise above adversity. When you finally come upon the creaking door marked "Redefinition," step through it boldly, leaving the catacombs behind and entering a garden of endless possibilities, where every setback is simply the prelude to a grand comeback.

Emerging from these halls, you will be emboldened, ready to face the world with a heart fortified by courage and a spirit unshaken by your past. The catacombs may have held you for a time, but now, you walk forward with the knowledge that failure is not the end—it's merely the beginning of a new, more powerful chapter in your story.

Room 12: The Basement of "I Can't Trust Anyone"

Descend into the dark, damp Basement of "I Can't Trust Anyone," where the walls are thick with cobwebs spun from past betrayals and broken promises. The floor creaks under the heavy weight of mistrust, and every corner harbor shadowy figures whispering tales of deceit. This room is filled with the chilling echoes of times when trust was shattered, leaving you guarded, wary, and hesitant to let anyone get too close.

But here is the twist—those shadows are not real; they are merely distorted memories that have taken on a life of their own, feeding off your fears. The belief that you can't trust anyone has trapped you in this basement, confining you to a space where isolation reigns and fear whispers in every crevice. To break free, you must begin the task of clearing away the cobwebs of old wounds, recognizing that while trust can be fragile, it is also the bedrock of meaningful connections.

Start small—take cautious steps toward allowing trust to rebuild. Let yourself trust in the little things, the simple gestures, and the everyday interactions. As you do, the basement will begin to brighten, the shadows will recede, and you will rediscover that not everyone is out to hurt you. The door to the basement isn't locked; it's simply been hidden behind layers of doubt. As you peel away these layers, you'll find the courage to step out into the light, ready to trust again, and open to the possibilities of new, genuine connections.

Room 13: The Attic of "I'll Never Be Happy"

At last, you ascend the creaky stairs to the Attic of "I'll Never Be Happy," a dusty, forgotten chamber where the remnants of abandoned dreams and unfulfilled desires linger like restless spirits. The air here is thick with resignation, and the grimy windows barely allow the faintest glimmer of light to seep in. This is a place where hope seems to have withered away, buried beneath the heavy belief that true happiness is a myth, always just out of reach, like a will-o'-the-wisp leading you deeper into the dark.

Yet, as you sift through the cobweb-covered boxes and discarded memories, you begin to see that this attic isn't as desolate as it first appeared. The notion that you'll never be happy is nothing more than a ghost story—one that's been whispered in the shadows for so long that it's begun to feel real. But like all ghost stories, it can be rewritten. Happiness isn't some elusive specter you stumble upon in the night—it's something you conjure, moment by moment, with each choice you make.

But before you can rewrite this story, ask yourself: Do you know what truly makes you happy? Are you chasing happiness like a phantom, always just out of reach, or do you recognize that it comes from within? Happiness isn't found in the approval of others or in distant, unattainable dreams—it's born from within, from living with purpose and embracing what genuinely makes your spirit dance.

To escape the attic, you must throw open the windows and let in the light, allowing it to chase away the shadows and reveal the truth: happiness is not a destination; it's the journey you embark on each day. When you focus on what puts a smile on your heart, happiness will follow you like a loyal phantom, ever-present and ever ready to illuminate your path.

It's time to dust off those forgotten dreams, reclaim your purpose, and start living the life that fills you with joy. Happiness isn't something you seek in the dark corners of the world—it's the light you carry within, guiding you through every twist and turn of your journey.

With these final rooms, your journey through the Haunted House of Negative Beliefs is complete. Each room has revealed the dark fears and doubts that have haunted you, but also the secrets to breaking free. From the grand hall of "I'm Not Good Enough," where the ghosts of past failures linger, to the attic of "I'll Never Be Happy," where forgotten dreams gather dust, you have faced the shadows that have long whispered lies in your ear.

You have descended into the crypt of "I'll Never Change," confronted the chilling Vault of "No One Loves Me," and navigated the treacherous Maze of "I Should Have Known Better." Each room, with its eerie atmosphere and unsettling reminders, was a test of your resilience and courage. But within these chambers, you also discovered the keys to your liberation—tools that can dismantle the chains of self-doubt and fear.

Armed with the knowledge and strategies of an Energy Vampire Blaster, you're now ready to leave this haunted house behind. The corridors of "They're Better Than Me" and the dungeon of "I'm Not Smart Enough" no longer hold sway over you. The attic windows have been flung open, letting in the light, and the shadows of mistrust in the basement of "I Can't Trust Anyone" have been banished.

As you step out of this house of horrors, you carry with you the wisdom to rewrite the narratives that once held you captive. The path ahead is no longer shrouded in darkness but illuminated with light, hope, and endless possibilities. The halls are now behind you, and the future is yours to create—a future where your spirit is unshaken, your heart is full, and your potential knows no bounds.

PART III

Energy Vampires Amongst Us

Venture deep into the dark forests of the outer world, where Energy Vampires hide in plain sight, masquerading as workplaces, toxic relationships, and draining social circles. But you, intrepid Energy Vampire Blaster, are no longer fooled by their tricks. Armed with the knowledge you have gained, you'll navigate these perilous environments, escape their clutches, and emerge stronger than ever.

Much Closer Than You Think!

The sinister corners of our lives where Energy Vampires lurk, waiting to sink their fangs into your vitality until you're left a mere shadow of your former self. These dark lairs aren't hidden away in ancient crypts or far-off castles. No, they're much closer than you'd like to think—perhaps in your workplace, your home, or even among your closest friends. But fear not, dear traveler, for once you learn to recognize the telltale signs of these energy-draining dens, you'll be well on your way to escaping their cold, clammy grip.

Prepare yourself as we descend into the heart of darkness, where the air is thick with dread, and the walls seem to close in with every step. These toxic environments fester and grow, and the longer you stay, the more they drain you, leaving you weak and weary. But with this guide, you'll learn to spot the red flags and, more importantly, find your way out before it's too late. So, light your lantern, sharpen your stake, and let's venture into the depths of The Vampire's Lair.

A Tour of Toxic Environments

As we step deeper into the shadows, the first thing you'll notice is how deceptively ordinary these lairs appear. That's part of their dark magic—they lure you in with a false sense of security before revealing their true, monstrous nature. Let's take a closer look at these cursed places:

The Soul-Sucking Workplace

Picture this: every morning, you step into your office, but instead of a place of productivity, it feels like you're walking into a haunted house. The air is thick with despair, and each tick of the clock sounds like a death knell. The office might look normal on the surface, but beneath it, it's teeming with Energy Vampires—coworkers who thrive on drama, bosses who sap your spirit with relentless demands, and a culture that's more toxic than a witch's brew. If the thought of Monday morning sends a chill down your spine, you might be trapped in a soul-sucking workplace.

In this lair, negativity hangs in the air like a thick fog, making it difficult to breathe. Every project becomes a battlefield, every meeting a horror show where creativity and motivation are bled dry. The Energy Vampires here are masters of manipulation, turning every interaction into a draining experience, leaving you feeling more like a zombie than a human by the end of the day.

To protect yourself in this cursed environment, you must set strong boundaries—your very own protective circle. Keep interactions professional and focused on work-related tasks, limiting your exposure to toxic coworkers. Seek out allies who share your values and can offer support, forming a coven of positivity amidst the chaos. And if the environment becomes unbearable, don't be afraid to explore new opportunities where your energy will be valued and respected.

Suffocating Relationships

Once upon a time, your relationship felt like a fairy tale, but now it's more of a horror story. You have wandered into the suffocating embrace of a vampire's lair, where love has turned into a nightmare. Your partner, once charming and sweet, has revealed their true nature—a controlling, manipulative force that drains you of your confidence and joy. You tiptoe around, trying to avoid triggering their wrath, but no matter what you do, it's never enough.

This lair is as confining as a coffin, with your partner acting as the vampire who slowly, methodically drains you of your self-worth. They use gaslighting to make you doubt your sanity and guilt-tripping to keep you in line. The walls close in, leaving you feeling trapped and helpless, as if the light at the end of the tunnel has been snuffed out.

To escape this suffocating coffin, you must reclaim your power. Carve out time for yourself, creating a sanctuary where the vampire's influence cannot reach. Speak your truth with the sharpness of a stake, clearly and assertively, letting them know where you stand. And if the darkness becomes too overwhelming, remember that seeking outside help is not a sign of weakness but a beacon of strength. Sometimes, the bravest thing you can do is to step back, reassess, and, if necessary, drive the final stake into the heart of the relationship, freeing yourself from its deathly grip.

The Negative Social Circle

The Negative Social Circle—a place where every gathering feels like a visit to the underworld. You walk in, hoping for a good time, but by the end, you feel like you have been dragged through the very depths of despair. In these toxic circles, the drama is endless, and the support is nonexistent. Recognizing these environments as harmful is the first step toward protecting your energy and reclaiming your peace.

Your so-called friends thrive on drama and gossip, their words dripping with envy and spite. Instead of lifting you up, they drag you down into the abyss, feeding off your energy like a pack of ravenous wolves. Every snide remark, every backhanded compliment, chips away at your confidence, leaving you questioning your worth.

To escape this lair, you must recognize the signs of a toxic social circle and take decisive action. Limit your interactions with those who thrive on negativity, and seek out relationships based on mutual respect, where support and encouragement replace jealousy and spite. Remember, your time and energy are precious—invest them in people who uplift you, not those who drag you down.

The Family Fortress

Even if you manage to break free from a suffocating relationship, the next challenge may lie within the walls of your own home. The Family Fortress can be a place of safety—or a stronghold for energy vampires who wield guilt and judgment as their weapons.

Venturing into the Family Fortress might feel like stepping into an ancient castle filled with hidden dungeons and secret passages, where family ties bind not just in love but in unspoken tension and expectations. The air is thick with the history of old grudges and the whispers of unsolicited advice. It seems every family gathering is less about joyous reunion and more about revisiting old wounds and reigniting familial feuds.

In this lair, you'll encounter subtle manipulations and overt criticisms from those who claim to know you best. Energy vampires in the family often disguise their draining ways under the guise of concern or 'tough love,' making it difficult to set boundaries without feeling guilty. Here, every conversation can feel like a minefield, where the wrong word could set off an emotional explosion. Parents or relatives may continuously recount tales of your past errors as if they were yesterday's news, keeping you tethered to a version of yourself you have long since evolved from.

To survive and thrive in the Family Fortress, you must arm yourself with strong emotional defenses. Be on the lookout for the traps of guilt-tripping and passive aggression, and counter them with calm confidence. Keep a sacred space within your heart, where no vampire's critique can reach.

Stick close to family members who lift your spirit, and don't hesitate to keep your distance from those who drain it. As you navigate the treacherous halls of the Family Fortress, wield the shield of your boundaries and the sword of your truth, knowing that you are the master of your own happiness—not their expectations.

Plotting Your Escape

In the twisted labyrinth of life, Energy Vampires lurk in the shadows, waiting to drain your spirit dry. But fear not, for you are now an apprentice of the Energy Vampire Blasters, armed with the knowledge and tools to protect your well-being with precision and confidence. You have identified the lair; you have spotted the vampires—and now it's time to plan your daring escape. Breaking free from a toxic environment isn't just a walk through a haunted house, but with the right strategies, you can banish these energy-sucking fiends and reclaim your vitality. Here's your survival guide to escaping the lair and stepping into the light:

Summon Your Allies: Seek Support

Even the bravest vampire hunter knows they can't face the darkness alone. Every slayer needs allies, whether it's a trusted friend, a wise mentor, or a sage therapist. These companions can offer the guidance, encouragement, and perspective you need as you navigate the treacherous path out of the lair. Remember, you don't have to fight the forces of darkness alone—there's strength in numbers, and your allies will help you banish those fiends for good.

Imagine a coven of trusted companions surrounding you, their combined strength forming a protective barrier against the creeping shadows. These are the people who see the real you, who understand your struggles, and who can help you decipher the dark riddles that keep you bound. Whether it's through shared wisdom, a shoulder to lean on, or practical advice, your allies are the torches that illuminate your path to freedom. Choose them wisely, for their support will be your shield against the darkest of nights.

Plot Your Escape: Develop an Exit Plan

If you're ensnared in a toxic workplace or trapped in a relationship that's draining the life out of you, you need a plan—an escape route mapped out with precision. This might mean updating your resume and casting your net wide in the job market, or it could involve seeking legal counsel or counseling to safely leave a harmful relationship. Like a seasoned vampire slayer, have a plan ready so that when the time comes, you can make a swift and confident exit—leaping through the window just as the first rays of dawn break through the darkness.

Picture yourself as the mastermind behind a great escape, every detail considered, every step calculated. Your exit plan is not just a list of actions but a blueprint for reclaiming your life. Begin by mapping out your current situation—where the traps are set, where the dangers lurk—and then chart your course toward freedom. The key is to be prepared, to anticipate the obstacles that may arise, and to have contingencies in place. Whether you're planning to leave a toxic job or an unhealthy relationship, your exit plan is your lifeline, your assurance that when the time comes, you'll be ready to break free.

Sharpen Your Stake: Practice Self-Care

The battle against Energy Vampires takes its toll, both mentally and physically. That's why self-care is as vital as sharpening your stake— it's your secret weapon in this ongoing fight. Engage in activities that recharge your energy, whether it's a brisk moonlit walk, meditation to clear the fog of the mind, or indulging in hobbies that bring joy back into your life. The stronger and more resilient you are, the better equipped you'll be to face down the vampires and emerge victorious.

Consider self-care as the ritualistic sharpening of your tools, preparing you for the challenges ahead. This is not about indulgence; it's about survival. Each act of self-care—be it a peaceful moment of reflection, a nourishing meal, or a creative outlet—fortifies your spirit, sharpening your resolve and renewing your strength. In the face of relentless negativity, these practices are your sanctuary, the moments when you gather your forces and prepare for the battles to come. Remember, a well-rested and centered vampire hunter is far more formidable than one who is weary and drained.

Trust Your Sixth Sense: Listen to Your Instincts

Never underestimate the power of your instincts—they are your most reliable weapon in this dark world. If something feels off, it probably is, and ignoring that gut feeling is like leaving the door wide open for the vampires to creep in. Your instincts are your internal compass, guiding you away from danger and toward safer, brighter places. In the eerie world of Energy Vampires, trust in your intuition is the difference between staying safe and getting caught in their traps.

Your sixth sense is the ancient magic that whispers warnings in the dark, the intuitive flash that guides you through the murk. It's the chill down your spine when something isn't right, the inner voice that urges caution when all seems well on the surface. Cultivate this sense, hone it like a blade, and trust it implicitly. When you feel that subtle tug of unease, heed it—your instincts are finely attuned to the unseen, detecting the dangers that lurk just beyond the edge of perception. By trusting in this inner guide, you stay one step ahead of the vampires, outmaneuvering their traps and slipping through their grasp.

Forge Your Armor: Build Resilience

Before you confront the outer darkness, fortify your inner defenses. Building resilience is akin to forging armor in the fires of your will. Start by nurturing a positive mindset that can transform obstacles into opportunities. Regularly engage in activities that boost your mental toughness, like challenging physical exercise or problem-solving games. Each challenge you overcome in your daily life builds resilience, preparing you to withstand the draining effects of Energy Vampires with greater fortitude.

Imagine donning a suit of gleaming armor, each piece forged in the crucible of your experiences. Your resilience is that armor, a shield against the slings and arrows of life's challenges. Every time you rise from a setback, every time you push through adversity, you are adding another layer of protection. This armor isn't just for show; it's a vital defense against the corrosive effects of doubt, fear, and negativity. Strengthen it with each victory, no matter how small, and know that with this armor, you can walk through the darkest of nights unscathed.

Redirect Negative Energy: Master the Art of Diversion

As you navigate through the vampire's lair, mastering the art of diversion can be your stealthiest tool. Learn to redirect negative interactions and energy into something positive. If faced with a toxic situation, change the subject or use humor to lighten the mood. By redirecting the flow of energy, you maintain control of the interaction, keeping the vampires disoriented and unable to feed on your energy.

Think of yourself as a skilled illusionist, capable of redirecting attention and energy with a flick of the wrist. When the vampires try to pull you into their web of negativity, you deftly shift the conversation, introduce a new perspective, or inject a bit of humor to defuse the tension. This isn't just about avoiding conflict; it's about reclaiming control over your interactions, ensuring that you remain the master of your own energy. By mastering the art of diversion, you become an unpredictable target, too slippery for the vampires to latch onto, leaving them frustrated and powerless.

Curate a Sanctuary of Safe Spaces

Every vampire hunter needs a haven, a sanctuary where they can retreat and recover. Cultivate such spaces both physically and mentally. Physically, arrange a part of your home to be a tranquil retreat where you can relax and rejuvenate away from the world's chaos. Mentally, develop a mindfulness or meditation practice that allows you to retreat into a calm inner sanctuary whenever external pressures mount. These sanctuaries are critical refuges where you can heal and gather strength for future encounters.

Envision your sanctuary as a sacred space, untouched by the darkness that prowls outside. This is your place of refuge, where the noise and chaos of the world cannot reach you. Fill it with objects, sounds, and scents that soothe your spirit and remind you of your strength. Whether it's a cozy corner of your home or a mental oasis you retreat to during meditation, this sanctuary is your fortress, your place of healing and renewal. Here, you can lay down your weapons, recharge your energy, and prepare for the battles ahead, knowing that within these walls, you are safe and whole.

Practice Rituals of Purification: Clear Negative Energy

Incorporate rituals of purification into your routine to cleanse yourself of any residual negativity from the vampire's lair. Practice deep breathing, salt baths with the glow of a candle, or smudge your home with sage to purify the energy fields. On a spiritual or emotional level, you might find it beneficial to write down negative experiences and burn the paper as a symbolic release. Regular purification rituals help maintain a clean, energetic slate, reducing the lingering influence of any encountered negativity.

Picture yourself as a powerful sorcerer, performing ancient rituals to banish the dark energies that cling to you after a long day. These rituals—whether physical, like a cleansing bath, or spiritual, like burning sage—are your way of resetting your energy, washing away the residue of negativity. Each act of purification is like sweeping away cobwebs, clearing the space for positive energy to flow freely. Make these rituals a part of your daily practice, a way to cleanse your aura and maintain your inner light, ensuring that the vampires' influence never takes root.

The Break of Dawn: Claiming Your Freedom

Armed with resilience, diversion tactics, a personal sanctuary, profound knowledge, and purification rituals, you stand ready not just to escape but to conquer the lair of Energy Vampires. As you implement these strategies, visualize the approaching dawn—the ultimate symbol of renewal and hope. With each step forward, the night recedes, and the first light of morning heralds a new day. This new beginning is your victory, earned through courage, wisdom, and unwavering determination. Now, step into the dawn as a beacon of light, empowered and free.

As the first rays of dawn pierce the darkness, feel the weight of the night lift from your shoulders. This is your moment of triumph, the culmination of all your efforts. The light of dawn symbolizes a new beginning, a fresh start untainted by the shadows of the past. As you step into this new day, carry with you the knowledge and strength you have gained, and let the light guide you forward. You have conquered the lair, banished the vampires, and now you are free—free to live a life filled with light, hope, and endless possibilities.

The Mirror of Self-Reflection

Before you confront the darkness that lurks in the lair, take a moment to gaze into the Mirror of Self-Reflection. This enchanted mirror reveals more than just your outer appearance—it shows the state of your inner world. Peer into its depths and ask yourself: Are there shadows within you that might be feeding the energy vampires around you? Perhaps you carry your own inner demons—habits, doubts, or fears—that need to be banished. Cleansing your soul of these energy leeches will strengthen your defenses, ensuring you're not only warding off external threats but also purifying the energy you project into the world. Polish your shield with self-awareness, and you'll be ready to face any vampire that crosses your path.

Step before the Mirror of Self-Reflection and dare to look deep within. This is no ordinary mirror—it shows you not just your face but your soul, reflecting back the hidden fears and doubts that may be feeding the vampires around you. As you confront these inner vampires, remember that acknowledging them is the first step to banishing them. Polish your shield of self-awareness until it gleams, casting light on even the darkest corners of your psyche. By cleansing your inner world, you strengthen your outer defenses, making you impervious to the vampires' grasp.

The Weapon of Gratitude

Gratitude is your secret weapon in the battle against the shadows. Like a blessed blade, it cuts through the fog of negativity that energy vampires thrive on. Each time you express gratitude, no matter how small, you create a spark of light that drives back the darkness. In the morning, reflect on the blessings that surround you, and let the warmth of thankfulness shield you throughout the day. At night, whisper words of appreciation before you sleep, and let them form a protective barrier in your dreams. This practice of gratitude is more than a ritual—it's a spell that fortifies your spirit, making it more difficult for vampires to sink their fangs into your soul.

Wield gratitude like a sacred weapon, its light cutting through the dense fog of negativity. Each expression of thanks is a spark, a small but potent spell that drives back the shadows and illuminates your path. Begin your day by counting your blessings, allowing the warmth of gratitude to shield you from the vampires' icy grip. As the day draws to a close, let words of appreciation form a barrier around you, guarding your dreams from the encroaching darkness. This simple yet powerful practice fortifies your spirit, ensuring that no vampire can dim your inner light.

The Beacon of Positivity

In a world filled with shadows, you have the power to be a Beacon of Positivity, drawing in good energy like a lighthouse guiding ships through a stormy night. By cultivating a radiant mindset, you attract allies and repel the darkness. Surround yourself with those who lift your spirits, engage in activities that make your soul sing, and let your light shine brightly. The more you nurture this inner glow, the stronger your defenses become, warding off the energy vampires who thrive in gloom. Remember, your light is not just for you—it's a guiding star for others who may be lost in the night.

Become a Beacon of Positivity, a shining light in the midst of the storm. Your positive energy is a powerful force, attracting allies and repelling the darkness. Cultivate this inner glow by surrounding yourself with people and activities that uplift your spirit, making your light shine even brighter. As your radiance grows, it forms a protective barrier around you, making it nearly impossible for the vampires to latch on. But remember, your light isn't just for you—it's a guiding star for others who may be lost in the night, helping them find their way back to safety.

The Healing Well

After the battle, you'll need to drink deeply from the Healing Well to restore your strength. This mystical well is filled with the waters of renewal, bubbling up from the depths of your own spirit. To draw from it, immerse yourself in the things that bring you peace and joy— whether it's wandering through a moonlit forest, losing yourself in the pages of a good book, or simply breathing in the quiet of dawn. Regularly returning to this well will keep your energy flowing, your spirit vibrant, and your defenses strong against any future threats. The Healing Well is your sanctuary, a place where you can return to replenish your reserves and emerge revitalized.

Descend to the Healing Well, where the waters of renewal await to restore your weary spirit. This well, deep and ancient, draws its power from within you, bubbling up with the essence of peace and joy. Each time you drink from these waters—be it through a quiet walk, a favorite book, or a moment of stillness—you replenish your strength, renewing your energy for the battles yet to come. The Healing Well is your sanctuary, a place of quiet power where you can retreat and recharge, emerging stronger and more vibrant with each visit.

The Crystal Ball

Finally, gaze into the Crystal Ball, where the mists of time part to reveal your future. This ancient tool of divination doesn't just show what is—it shows what could be, based on the energy you project into the world. As you peer into its depths, focus on the bright future you wish to create, filled with positivity, love, and success. The visions you conjure within the Crystal Ball are more than mere dreams—they are the first steps in manifesting your destiny. With each positive thought and intention, you shape the mist into reality, guiding your journey toward a future where energy vampires hold no sway over your life.

Peer into the Crystal Ball, where the mists swirl and part to reveal the future you are creating. This is not a passive vision but an active process, where your thoughts, intentions, and energy shape what is to come. As you focus on the bright future you desire—one filled with love, success, and positivity—the mist begins to solidify, turning dreams into reality. The Crystal Ball is your tool of manifestation, a way to guide your journey toward a future free from the grasp of energy vampires. With each positive thought, you carve out a path through the mist, leading you to a life of light and endless possibility.

Reclaiming Your Energy

As you journey through the corridors of life, remember that you hold the power to banish the shadows and reclaim your light. Escaping the Vampire's Lair is no small feat, but with each step you take, each boundary you set, and each empowering choice you make, you weaken the grip of those who seek to drain your spirit. The battle may be fierce, but the reward is a life filled with vitality, joy, and purpose. You have armed yourself with knowledge, sharpened your tools, and fortified your defenses—now, it's time to take action. The path to freedom is illuminated by the dawn of a new day, where the darkness of the past gives way to the brilliant light of your empowered future. So, step boldly into the light, for you are the master of your fate, and the shadows no longer have any hold over you.

"No" Is Your Most Potent Spell

Under the soft glow of the moon, when you find yourself surrounded by Energy Vampires, fear not, for mastering the art of saying "no" with confidence and clarity is the most potent spell in your arsenal. This simple word, when wielded with intent and precision, can protect your energy and preserve your well-being like a magical barrier that no vampire can breach.

The Spell of Declination

The ability to say "no" is like choosing between trick or treat at a ghostly banquet. Energy Vampires thrive on your hesitation, your inability to refuse their demands. But you, equipped with the wisdom of this chapter, will learn to offer a "trick" (a polite but firm refusal) or a "treat" (a clever redirection or alternative) to safeguard your energy. By casting this spell of declination, you maintain control over your time and emotional resources, preventing these vampires from sinking their fangs into your life force.

Brewing the Perfect Response

Let's descend into the eerie mists of common scenarios and discover how to conjure the perfect response to guard your energy from those pesky Energy Vampires:

The Social Jester (Social Events)

Picture yourself at a ghoulish gathering, when a Drama Queen swoops in, desperate to drag you into their swirling vortex of chaos. Instead of getting ensnared in their web, you flash a mischievous smile and say, "I'm here to enjoy the night; let's catch up another time." With that, you have cast a deflective spell, one that shields your joy and sends their neediness spiraling into the shadows. Your energy remains intact, allowing you to revel in the eerie delights of the evening, unbothered by their dark drama.

The Workplace Wraith (Work Demands)

Imagine your boss, a true Workplace Wraith, trying to load your cauldron with even more tasks than it can brew. You respond with a polite yet firm incantation: "I'm focused on current projects; perhaps someone else can take this on?" This redirection is a spell of self-preservation, ensuring you stay in control of your workload without being consumed by the relentless demands of the office dungeon. With this spell, you stave off the specter of burnout and keep your power firmly in your own hands.

The Domestic Dungeon (Home Life)

At home, if a family member constantly leans on you like a ghoul seeking to drain your emotional reserves, you might gently invoke, "I need some time to recharge; let's talk later." This spell of protection sets a boundary while still showing care, ensuring your energy is safeguarded. By casting this spell, you create a barrier that prevents your vitality from being sapped by the constant demands of others. Your energy is yours to keep, and this gentle enchantment ensures it stays that way.

Techniques for Firm Boundaries

The Mirror Shield

When an Energy Vampire tries to latch onto your life force, visualize a protective mirror forming around you, reflecting their demands back at them. This magical shield keeps their negativity at bay while you remain composed and firm. A strong "no" delivered with calm assurance becomes your ultimate defense. This Mirror Shield is your magical defense against the creeping encroachments of those who seek to drain your energy.

The Mantle of Clarity

Clarity is your sharpest weapon when setting boundaries. Be as direct as a witch's hex, with no room for negotiation. For instance, "I can't take this on right now," is a spell that leaves no openings for further discussion. Wrap yourself in the Mantle of Clarity, and your message will be understood, respected, and unchallenged by those who might try to push your limits. This magical garment ensures your boundaries remain unbreached.

The Cloak of Kindness

Even the darkest refusals can be cloaked in kindness. When declining, wrap your words in a gentle spell: "I appreciate you thinking of me, but I can't help this time." This soft yet powerful enchantment allows you to maintain respect while holding firm. The Cloak of Kindness ensures your "no" is delivered without stirring animosity, letting you protect your energy while keeping the peace.

With these spells at your disposal, you're now equipped to banish the Energy Vampires from your life and keep your precious energy safe from their draining grasp.

Overcoming the Fear of Saying No

In the eerie, moonlit landscape of life, the thought of saying "no" can feel as daunting as facing a ghostly apparition. But fear not, for the courage to protect your energy is within your grasp.

Potion of Courage: Picture yourself as an alchemist in a shadowy tower, brewing a potion of strength. Recall past moments where you successfully set boundaries—each memory a powerful ingredient that bubbles with confidence. Stir in affirmations like, "I have the right to protect my time and energy," to enhance the brew. With every sip of this potion, your ability to say "no" grows stronger, your resolve fortified against the dark forces that seek to drain you.

Gather Support: Just as witches gather in covens to amplify their power, so too should you seek the company of trusted allies. Share your challenges with friends or mentors who can lend their strength to yours. Their support will bolster your confidence, making your "no" as potent as any spell cast under a full moon. Together, your collective energy forms a protective circle, warding off those who seek to weaken your defenses.

Protecting Your Energy: In the shadowed halls of relationships, balance is key. If you find yourself constantly giving without receiving, it's time to invoke the Barrier of Balanced Exchange. This magical practice ensures that your generosity is not exploited, maintaining your energy at healthy levels. This ward acts as a shield, safeguarding you from one-sided interactions that leave you drained and vulnerable.

But sometimes, even the most fortified barriers need reinforcement. Enter the **Shield of Solitude**—a mystical refuge where you can retreat and recharge. This is not a place of loneliness, but a sanctuary of peace, where you can reconnect with your inner strength, far from the prying eyes and grasping hands of Energy Vampires. Whether it's a quiet nook in your home or a moment of serene reflection, solitude is where your spirit can restore its vitality, preparing you to face the world once more.

The Festival of Freedoms

With these enchanted tools at your disposal, you step forward into a world where you are no longer at the mercy of Energy Vampires. The art of saying "no" is your most powerful spell, a charm that preserves your vitality and joy. Embrace this newfound freedom and let each "no" be a flame that lights your path through the darkness, keeping the vampires at bay. Celebrate this Festival of Freedoms, where your empowered choices shine like lanterns in the night, guiding you to a life filled with light and purpose. Your energy is precious. Guard it well, and watch as your life blossoms under the protection of your self-assured "no."

Energy Vampire Blasting Spells

20 Magical Phrases to Keep Your Energy Intact

When you feel your energy is being drained speak any of these potions in your mind or out loud and it will help you deflect the negativity.

Guarding and Deflecting:

"Not my vampire, not my energy."

"I guard my energy, casting away your shadows."

"I deflect your negativity, reclaiming my light."

"I cast away your influence, denying you power over me."

"I guard my peace, deflecting your draining presence."

"I deny your entry into my thoughts, casting away your energy."

"My light is guarded, your shadows have no place here."

"I deflect your attempts to drain me, standing strong in my power."

"I guard my soul, casting away all that does not serve me."

"Your energy cannot penetrate my shield; I deflect it with ease."

Potions of Forgiveness and Release

"I forgive and release you, reclaiming my power."

"I forgive and release your influence over my energy."

"I forgive and release your shadows, embracing my light."

"I forgive and release the past, casting away your hold on me."

"I forgive and release you, restoring my peace and strength."

"I forgive and release your negativity, reclaiming my joy."

"I forgive and release your toxic hold, embracing my freedom."

"I forgive and release your energy, returning it to the void."

"I forgive and release all negativity, standing in my power."

"I forgive and release, denying your shadows any influence over me."

Potions of Empowerment

"I reclaim my power, casting away your influence."

"I deny your negativity, standing tall in my strength."

"I cast away your energy, embracing my own light."

"I stand strong, denying your attempts to drain me."

"My energy is my own, I deflect your shadows."

"I cast away your influence, reclaiming my peace."

"I deny your power over me, standing firm in my light."

"I deflect your negativity, keeping my energy pure."

"I cast away your attempts to drain me, guarding my joy."

"I deny your entry, my energy is my fortress."

Potions for Warding off Energy Vampires

Even the most seasoned witch or wizard needs a few tricks up their sleeve to keep Energy Vampires at bay. Here are some fun and easy "potions" you can cast to protect your energy and keep those draining forces from sucking the life out of you.

The Circle of Salt Shielding Spell

"With salt, I protect, with a circle, I deflect."

What You'll Need:

- Coarse sea salt

- A little bit of sage (dried or essential oil)

- A space to create a small circle (around your workspace or yourself)

How to Cast the Spell:

1. **Sprinkle some salt** in a circle around your workspace or where you're sitting. Picture a glowing barrier of light forming around you as you do.

2. **Add a pinch of sage** (or a drop of sage oil) within the circle to clear out any lingering negativity.

3. **Say the words** and imagine this circle as an invisible shield that keeps out negativity and energy-draining vibes.

4. **Step into the circle** (physically or mentally) and feel protected as you go about your day.

This spell is great when you're about to dive into a meeting, family dinner, or any situation where you feel your energy might get zapped.

The Reflective Mirror Charm

"Mirror, mirror in my hand, reflect the vibes I can't withstand."

What You'll Need:

- A small handheld mirror

- Lavender oil

- A white candle

How to Cast the Spell:

1. **Dab a little lavender oil** around the edges of your mirror to keep things calm and soothing.

2. **Light the white candle** and let its light purify the space.

3. **Hold the mirror up** and picture it is bouncing any bad vibes right back to where they came from.

4. **Recite the rhyme** to empower the mirror with protective magic.

5. **Keep the mirror** with you or place it facing outward near your workspace or home entrance.

Use this spell when you're about to face someone who tends to drain your energy or when you need a little extra protection in a difficult situation.

The Incantation of Energetic Armor

"In light or dark, my energy stays bright, wrapped in armor of glowing light."

What You'll Need:

- A piece of black tourmaline or obsidian (or any stone you feel drawn to)

- Your favorite piece of clothing (your "armor")

- A quiet moment to gather your thoughts

How to Cast the Spell:

1. **Hold the stone** in your hand and let its grounding energy settle you.

2. **As you put on your clothes**, imagine them glowing with a protective light, like magical armor.

3. **Say the incantation**, feeling the light grow stronger around you.

4. **Wear your 'armor'** throughout the day, knowing you're shielded from any energy vampires lurking around.

Perfect for days when you know you'll be in energy-draining situations or just need a little extra boost of confidence.

The Circle of Fiery Defense

"Fire bright, guard my might, keep me safe through day and night."

What You'll Need:

- Red candles

- Cinnamon oil

- A safe space to set up the circle

How to Cast the Spell:

1. **Set up the candles** in a circle around where you'll be sitting.

2. **Anoint each candle** with cinnamon oil to ignite the energy of fire and protection.

3. **Light the candles one by one**, reciting the incantation as you go.

4. **Sit within the circle**, letting the fiery energy shield you from harm.

This spell is your go-to when you're about to face a particularly tough challenge or confrontation

The Binding Braid of Banishment

"Braid of power, set me free, bind away what's draining me."

What You'll Need:

- Three strands of yarn or ribbon (different colors)

- A small lock of your hair

- A quiet place

How to Cast the Spell:

1. **Braid the three strands together**, incorporating a small lock of your hair for a personal touch.

2. **Chant the spell** as you braid, focusing on binding and banishing negative energy away from you.

3. **Bury the braid** in the earth or keep it with you as a talisman.

This spell is especially helpful when you're dealing with persistent negativity and need to keep it at bay for the long haul.

Each spell is designed not just to ward off unwanted energies but to empower you with a sense of magical control over your own space and well-being. Add these spells to your Book of Spells and watch as your arsenal against Energy Vampires becomes more formidable by the night.

Embracing Your Inner Guardian

Warding off Energy Vampires isn't something for the meek or those who would rather hide under the covers than confront their fears. No, this requires grit, a pinch of moxie, and a good dose of eerie enchantments. With the right set of mystical rituals and a steely resolve, you can shield your essence and keep those nefarious energy suckers trembling in the mist.

By casting your protective circle, intricately carving your jack-o'-lantern (sharp tools required, beware!), summoning your circle of allies, conjuring talismans of power, igniting the white flame candle, and chronicling your exploits in your very own Book of Spells, you're equipped to face down any parasitic presence that dares drift into your realm.

Recall, you are the stalwart guardian of your energy, the overseer of your enchanted enclave, and the defender of your soul's sanctuary. The rituals you have unearthed here are no mere child's play—they are formidable spells, steeped in ancient lore, that when wielded with regularity, fortify you against the creeping shadows.

So, stand firm, ignite your candle with a spark, and march into the night with audacity and a wry smirk. Armed with your arcane arsenal, let every Energy Vampire know they've met their match. Hold your ground, fearless spellbinders, and send those Energy Vampires scurrying back into the darkness!

The Graveyard of Past Mistakes

Step softly as we enter the hallowed grounds of the Graveyard of Past Mistakes. Here, amid the eerie whispers of regret and the chilling wind of remorse, the phantoms of bygone errors float ceaselessly. These specters can haunt your every step, sapping your energy with their mournful wails of what might have been. But fear not! For within these pages lies the secret to silencing these ghosts—permitting you to forgive yourself, bury your mistakes, and stride forward with renewed vigor.

Ritual for Releasing Regrets

To free yourself from the clutches of these restless spirits, you must perform the ancient and solemn Burial Ceremony—a rite that symbolically lays your past errors to eternal rest.

Gathering the Ghosts (Identifying Your Mistakes): Begin by summoning the spirits of your past mistakes. Reflect on each, not with self-castigation but with the objective eye of a necromancer assessing the spirits in his charge. Write them down on pieces of parchment—each a tombstone in waiting.

Words of Release (Writing Forgiveness Letters): For each ghost, pen a letter of forgiveness. Address the letter to yourself, detailing the mistake, acknowledging the lessons learned, and explicitly forgiving yourself. This act of writing is a powerful spell of release, breaking the chains that bind these specters to your soul.

The Lighting of Candles (Setting Intentions for Moving Forward): As dusk falls over the graveyard, light a candle for each past mistake. The flame represents your inner light—the power of your spirit burning brighter than the shadows of past regrets. As you light each candle, set an intention to move forward, letting the light guide your path out of the darkness.

Burying the Parchments (A Physical Act of Letting Go): With a spade in hand and resolve in your heart, bury each parchment in the earth. As you cover them with soil, visualize burying your regrets, allowing them to decompose and enrich the soil of your future growth. This act is both physical and symbolic, grounding your commitment to move forward in the fertile earth of newfound wisdom.

Chanting the Spells of Renewal: As you stand over the freshly filled graves, chant spells of renewal and rebirth. These can be simple affirmations or elaborate incantations, such as, "From the earth, new growth arises, from my regrets, new strength is born."

The Elixir of Inner Peace: Embracing Self-Forgiveness

As any seasoned alchemist knows, the most potent elixirs are those brewed within. The Elixir of Inner Peace is one such potion, crafted not from herbs or minerals, but from the profound acceptance of your own human imperfections:

Brewing the Potion (Practicing Self-Compassion): Daily, mix a dose of self-compassion. Remind yourself that to err is not just human, but a part of the grand adventure of life. Each mistake is a misstep on the path to wisdom.

Adding Ingredients of Perspective: Sprinkle in the understanding that each past error has contributed to the depth of your character and the breadth of your experience. These ingredients help dilute the bitterness of regret.

Daily Consumption: Drink this elixir each morning to fortify yourself against the day's challenges and to remind yourself that you are more than the sum of your past missteps.

Dancing on the Graves of Regrets

With the burial ceremony complete and the Elixir of Inner Peace coursing through your veins, feel the weight of your regrets lighten. Dance upon the graves of your past mistakes not in disrespect, but in liberation—celebrating your freedom from their chains. As you leave the graveyard behind, carry forward the lessons learned but leave the ghosts to their eternal rest. The night is dark, but your path is lit with the candles of insight, and your steps are sure with the power of forgiveness.

Illumination with Gratitude and Forgiveness

In the shadowy corridors where Energy Vampires lurk, the ultimate Blasters at your disposal are Gratitude and Forgiveness. These powerful forces don't just repel the darkness; they transform it, illuminating your path and restoring peace to your spirit. Gratitude and Forgiveness are not merely defenses; they are the most potent tools in your arsenal, capable of turning even the darkest energy into light. Let's delve into how these mystical energies can fortify your defenses and rejuvenate your soul.

Gratitude: The Radiant Beacon

Gratitude acts as a luminous beacon, piercing through the oppressive gloom cast by Energy Vampires. When you focus on the blessings in your life, you shift from dwelling on deficits to celebrating the abundance that surrounds you. This alchemy doesn't ignore life's trials; instead, it highlights the treasures often obscured by them.

Practicing gratitude is akin to donning spectacles that filter out the bleak and amplify the bright. Amidst a gathering of ghouls, it's your personal shield, repelling the pessimism and despair that these creatures thrive on. Gratitude doesn't just ward off negativity; it elevates your entire being, making you less susceptible to the draining forces of the outer world.

Unleashing the Power of the Gratitude Blaster:

Morning and Evening Rituals: Start and end your day by conjuring thoughts of gratitude—your first and last spells of the day. As dawn breaks, summon a simple thought: What are you grateful for today? This sets your day aglow with protective light, casting away shadows and keeping those lurking malevolent forces at bay. When night falls, reflect on the blessings that have crept into your day, no matter how small. These daily rituals weave an aura of positivity around you, one that Energy Vampires cannot pierce.

The Gratitude Ledger: Keep a sacred tome, your Gratitude Ledger, where you inscribe daily entries of thanks. This ongoing ritual builds a fortress of positivity, shielding you from the draining energies that prowl the outer world. With each word you write, your resolve strengthens, your spirit brightens, and your gratitude transforms into a powerful force—one that wards off negativity with ease.

Benedictions of Appreciation: Regularly cast your gratitude upon others—these are your Benedictions of Appreciation. This practice not only fortifies your relationships but also creates an aura of positivity that repels any negative intrusions. Gratitude, when shared, multiplies, forming a glowing network of light that makes it harder for Energy Vampires to thrive in your presence.

With the Gratitude Blaster in hand, you'll find your energy protected, your spirit fortified, and your path illuminated, no matter what dark forces may lurk in the shadows.

Forgiveness: The Key to Unshackling the Spirit

Forgiveness is the ultimate enchantment for releasing the chains of resentment that bind you to the past. Clinging to old grievances grants Energy Vampires free reign over your emotional realm, continually sapping your vitality. Choosing to forgive cuts these binds, not condoning the wrongdoing, but liberating you from its weight.

Forgiveness is a potent spell of liberation—it doesn't erase the past but disempowers it. By letting go of resentment, you reclaim the energy that was once drained by anger and bitterness. Forgiveness allows you to move forward, unburdened by the heavy chains of the past, making you resilient and impervious to the parasitic nature of Energy Vampires.

Wielding the Mighty Forgiveness Blaster

Self-Forgiveness: Often, the most formidable dungeon is the one we construct for ourselves. Release yourself from self-imposed captivity by forgiving your own missteps. Recognize that holding onto self-blame only feeds the Energy Vampires within, weakening your resolve. Forgive yourself as you would a dear friend, allowing compassion to dissolve the barriers to your inner strength.

Ritual of Release: Recognize the hurts inflicted by others, then consciously choose to let them go. This might require a private ceremony where you symbolically (or literally) burn the grievances, watching the smoke carry away the weight of your woes. This ritual not only frees you but also sends a clear message to the Energy Vampires that their influence has been nullified.

Unconditional Release: True forgiveness does not wait on the transgressor's remorse. Free yourself on your own terms, independent of their actions, to reclaim your power. This act of release transforms your energy field, turning it into a sanctuary where negativity cannot dwell.

The Synergy of Light: Gratitude and Forgiveness

Together, Gratitude and Forgiveness form a formidable duo against the darkness of Energy Vampires. Gratitude illuminates your path, while Forgiveness clears the debris of past battles. This combination not only shields you but also transforms your environment, attracting more light and less darkness.

These practices do more than just protect—they actively neutralize the energy-draining vibes of Energy Vampires. Gratitude keeps you focused on the positive, making it difficult for negative energies to take hold. Forgiveness frees up your emotional and spiritual space, ensuring that past wounds don't fester and provide a feeding ground for Energy Vampires.

Embrace these practices not as occasional spells but as daily rituals. Begin each day by charging your spirit with gratitude and end by cleansing it with forgiveness. Over time, you will notice a profound transformation not only in your resilience against energy vampires but in the very quality of your energy and life.

Thus, armed with Gratitude and Forgiveness, stride confidently through the shadowed realms. These tools do more than protect— they transmute darkness into light, sorrow into joy, and conflict into peace. Welcome them into your daily walk, and watch as the very atmosphere around you brightens, repelling the dark forces and drawing ever closer to the life of light you are meant to lead.

The Coven of Light

Embracing Your Tribe and Seeking Wise Mentors

As the final chapter of our journey through the haunted halls and shadowy paths of life unfolds, it's time to step into the light with newfound wisdom and strength. You have faced the Energy Vampires, fortified your spirit, and now, as a true Halloween Energy Vampire Blaster, there's one last treasure to uncover—the power of the people you choose to surround yourself with.

In every great tale of adventure, the hero never walks alone. Whether it's a band of brave companions or a wise mentor guiding the way, the journey is always richer, the victories sweeter, and the battles less daunting when you have the right people by your side. This chapter is your invitation to build your own coven of light—a group of souls who uplift, inspire, and illuminate your path.

The Power of Your Coven

Imagine your life as a grand, enchanted castle. The people you allow inside its walls are not mere visitors—they are the ones who help you guard the gates, polish the armor, and light the torches that keep the darkness at bay. The company you keep affects everything—your health, your happiness, your wealth, and your overall quality of life. The right people can elevate your spirit, ignite your dreams, and help you grow in ways you never imagined.

But beware, for not all who seek entrance to your castle come with pure intentions. Some may be disguised as friends, yet drain your energy, dim your light, and sow seeds of doubt in your heart. That is why it's crucial to choose your companions wisely, to protect your inner circle with the same care and vigilance you have used to repel the Energy Vampires from your life.

Surround yourself with those who celebrate your victories, support you in your struggles, and encourage you to reach for the stars. These are the members of your coven of light—your tribe, your family of choice, who will stand with you through every storm and help you shine even brighter.

The Wisdom of Mentors and Guides

As you journey forward, never underestimate the value of a wise mentor. In every great tale, there is always a sage figure, a wizard, or a guide who helps the hero navigate the unknown, offering wisdom that can only come from experience. In your own story, seeking out mentors—those who have walked the path before you—can make all the difference.

A mentor is like a lantern in the dark, casting light on the twists and turns ahead. They've faced the same challenges, battled their own Energy Vampires, and emerged stronger. Their guidance can help you avoid pitfalls, seize opportunities, and grow into the person you're destined to become.

But remember, just as you seek out mentors, be open to becoming a guide for others as well. The wisdom you have gained on this journey can illuminate the way for those who follow. Share your light, your knowledge, and your experiences, and you will find that teaching others deepens your own understanding and strengthens your own resolve.

The Magic of Connection

In the end, the magic of life lies in the connections we make. The people who walk beside us, the mentors who guide us, and the community we build are the true treasures of our journey. As you step out of the shadows and into the light, cherish these connections. Nurture them, protect them, and allow them to grow.

Your life is a grand adventure, and the people you choose to bring along for the ride will make all the difference. So, choose wisely, seek out wisdom, and never walk the path alone. Together, with your coven of light and the guidance of wise mentors, you will continue to grow, to shine, and to thrive.

Congratulations, dear Halloween Energy Vampire Blaster—you have not only reclaimed your energy, but you have also discovered the true power of community, mentorship, and connection. The journey may continue, but with your coven by your side and mentors to light the way, there's nothing you cannot achieve.

Let your light shine bright, and may your path be ever illuminated by the warmth of those who walk with you.

The End... and the Beginning

This is not just the end of our tale, but the beginning of a new chapter in your life—a chapter filled with light, love, and the power of positive connections. Embrace it with all your heart, and remember, the best is yet to come.

Afterword

The Final Showdown

Celebrating Your Power and Embracing the Light

As the moon dips below the horizon, signaling the end of this eerie journey, you stand triumphant at the edge of the darkness, having conquered the 13 Energy Vampires that once possessed your life. You have navigated the twisted labyrinths of your mind, confronted the shadowy figures that drained your spirit, and emerged as a true Halloween Energy Vampire Blaster. But beware—this is not the final page of your tale. It's merely the beginning of your empowered life.

Throughout daring adventure, you have learned to identify the vampires lurking in the shadows, mastered the art of setting boundaries, and fortified your defenses with self-care, resilience, and the power of a well-placed "no." These tools are more than mere weapons for battle—they are the keys to unlocking a life brimming with vitality, joy, and light.

As you step into the dawn of your newfound freedom, remember that the true power of a Halloween Energy Vampire Blaster lies not just in the battles won, but in the wisdom to maintain your light in the face of lingering darkness. The vampires may return, donning new disguises, but you are now armed with the insight and strength to recognize and repel them. Trust your instincts, wield your gratitude and positivity like the enchanted tools they are, and choose your companions wisely. For the most important decision you will ever make is the people you allow into your life.

The people around you have a profound impact on your health, happiness, wealth, standard of living, the home you dwell in, the carriage you ride, and your overall quality of life. Remember, Energy Vampires are not bad people—they're simply living out their stories, shaped by their own upbringing and traumas. They're learning their lessons, just as you have learned yours. Yet, you must be the gatekeeper of your realm, selecting those who uplift and nourish your spirit.

This journey hasn't just been about banishing the vampires; it's been about reclaiming your energy, your life, and your right to shine. As you move forward, let your light be a beacon for those still trapped in the shadows, guiding them toward their own liberation.

So, as you close this book and return to your world, carry with you the lessons learned and the strength gained. You are no longer a victim of the vampires that once sapped your energy. You are a warrior of light, a master of your own energy, and a beacon of hope in a world that can sometimes feel as dark as the deepest night.

Embrace your power, continue to grow, and let your light shine brighter than ever before. The night may be long, but you are the dawn. And with each new day, you rise stronger, wiser, and more vibrant, ready to face whatever comes your way. Congratulations, Halloween Energy Vampire Blaster—your journey to reclaiming your power has only just begun. Choose your allies with care, for they are the ones who will help you keep your light blazing, even in the darkest of times.

A Spooky Thank You from David Strauss

Dear Brave Soul,

As you reach the final page of this unearthly journey, I want to take a moment to extend my deepest gratitude to you. Yes, you—the courageous reader who dared to venture into the lairs of the 13 Energy Vampires, armed with nothing but your curiosity and a desire to reclaim your power. Together, we've navigated the twists and turns of this eerie path, faced the ghosts of toxic relationships, and emerged on the other side stronger, wiser, and perhaps even a little more mischievous.

Thank you for allowing me to be your guide through this dark and enchanted world. It's not every day that one gets to share such a spooky adventure with a kindred spirit, and I'm honored that you chose to walk this path with me. Your willingness to confront your fears, to laugh at the absurdity of it all, and to embrace the power within you has been nothing short of inspiring.

Writing this book was a journey in itself, filled with the same highs and lows, twists and turns that you have experienced as a reader. And knowing that these words have found their way to someone as bold and resilient as you fill my heart with a warmth that even the coldest of shadows can't diminish.

I hope that as you close this book, you carry with you not just the lessons we've uncovered, but also the lightness of spirit that comes from giggling in the face of the unknown. Remember, life is as much about the laughs as it is about the challenges, and sometimes, the best way to banish those pesky energy vampires is to simply giggle them away.

So, here's to you—to your courage, your spirit, and your endless capacity for growth. May you continue to blast away the shadows in your life, to embrace the light within you, and to giggle your way through every twist and turn that lies ahead.

From the bottom of my grateful heart, thank you for being a part of this journey. You have made it unforgettable.

With BIG LOVE, BIG gratitude, and warmest wishes,

David Strauss

Just Giggle

The Final Trick in the Halloween Spell book

There's something spellbindingly liberating about reaching the end of your journey with the 13 Energy Vampires, standing victorious on the other side of all that emotional turmoil, and just... giggling. Yes, giggling! But this isn't just any ordinary sound—it's the kind of witchy cackle that bubbles up from the cauldron of your soul, infused with the innocent joy of a child discovering a secret spell book for the first time.

Giggling isn't just a reaction; it's something far more magical, more intimate. It's that uncontrollable, effervescent burst of joy that seems to rise from the very depths of your spirit, much like the unexpected puff of smoke from a well-cast spell. While other forms of expression can be loud, shared among a coven in response to a good jest, giggling is personal, often shared between close companions or savored alone, like a cherished charm. It's the kind of sound that lights up the room with its purity, chasing away the shadows with its simplicity.

Giggling has a way of breaking down the walls of even the most broken hearts, connecting us to a time when joy was unfiltered, free from the curses of adulthood. It's a reminder that, at our core, there's a part of us that remains untouched by life's darker spells—a part that finds delight in the simplest of things, much like a young witch discovering the world's enchantments for the first time.

Giggling is the heart's way of whispering, "It's okay to let go and just be." It's about looking back at the ghastly rollercoaster of toxic relationships, the drama, the highs and lows, and finding the humor in the fact that, well, we played the starring role in our own supernatural soap operas. This chapter is an ode to the art of letting go, forgiving ourselves, and embracing the power of giggling through the practice of Giggle Yoga.

Imagine realizing that the key to unlocking your emotional chains wasn't held by some nefarious ghoul, but by you all along. That's right—it was your own thoughts, beliefs, fears, doubts, judgments, and sky-high expectations that crafted the spooky script of your past relationships. It's like discovering you have been the witch in charge of your own drama without even knowing it. And when this realization hits, what can you do but giggle?

Giggle Yoga isn't about contorting yourself into a pretzel while cackling like a maniacal witch (though, if that's your thing, go for it!). It's a metaphorical practice, a way of life that involves looking at your reflections, your missteps, and your 'what was I thinking?' moments with a light heart. It's giggling at the absurdity of our human experience, at the ways we complicate love, and at the sheer comedy of realizing we've had the power to change the channel all along.

Taking 100% responsibility for our lives, with no room for blame or victimhood, is incredibly empowering. It's acknowledging that every choice, every reaction, and every belief was ours to conjure. And while that might seem as daunting as facing a horde of zombies, there's a peculiar strength that comes from owning our part in our stories. It's a strength that's best celebrated with a giggle.

Why giggle, you ask? Because giggling is the perfect antidote to toxicity. It's impossible to hold onto anger, resentment, or sadness when you're genuinely giggling from the belly of your soul. Giggling brings us back to the present, to the simplicity of the moment, and reminds us that life, in all its complexity, is also ridiculously funny.

So, as you step forward from your spooky detox, carry with you the lightness of a giggle. Forgive yourself for the times you forgot your worth, for when you let fear guide your steps, and for those moments when you thought you needed someone else to complete you. Forgive, let go, and giggle at the beautiful messiness of being human.

As you practice Giggle Yoga, remember to giggle not just at yourself but at the collective comedy of human relationships. We're all stumbling, casting spells, and learning the mysterious dance of love. And when we can share a giggle over our shared follies, we find a common ground more solid and healing than any romantic potion.

In the end, "Just Giggle" is more than just a chapter title—it's an invitation. An invitation to lighten up, to find joy in the journey, and to celebrate the incredible resilience of the human heart with giggling. So, take a deep breath, look back at your path with kindness and humor, and let your heart giggle. Because sometimes, giggling truly is the best potion.

*There arrives a moment in life
when you step back from the chaos
and those who brew it.*

*Choose to be around those
who bring joy and laughter.*

*Let go of negativity
and cherish the positive.*

*Embrace those who care for you,
and wish well for those who don't.*

Life's too fleeting to not embrace joy.

*Stumbling is inevitable in life,
but rising again is truly living.*

It is your life.

Rise and shine.

—David Lloyd Strauss

Write That Book Already

Let David Strauss help you write and publish your book!

Author Coaching · Ghost Writing

Editing · Publishing

Done for you OR Done with you!

Go to: DavidStrauss.com

David's Other Books

David's 2nd Book

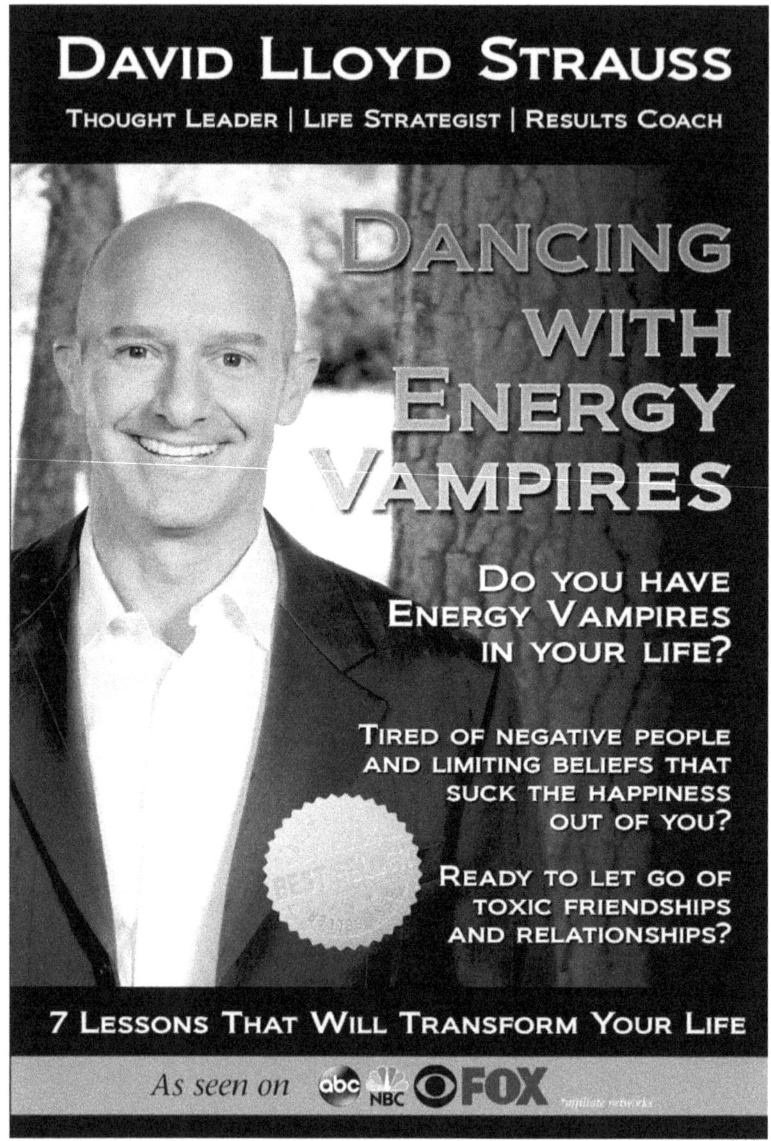

David's 3rd Book

SECOND MOUSE GETS THE CHEESE

FEELING TRAPPED BY MISTAKES, BAD ADVICE OR INEXPERIENCE?

Upgrade your thinking
Make smarter decisions
Build strong relationships

DAVID LLOYD STRAUSS

David's 4th Book

David's 5th Book

David's 6th Book

David's 7ᵗʰ Book

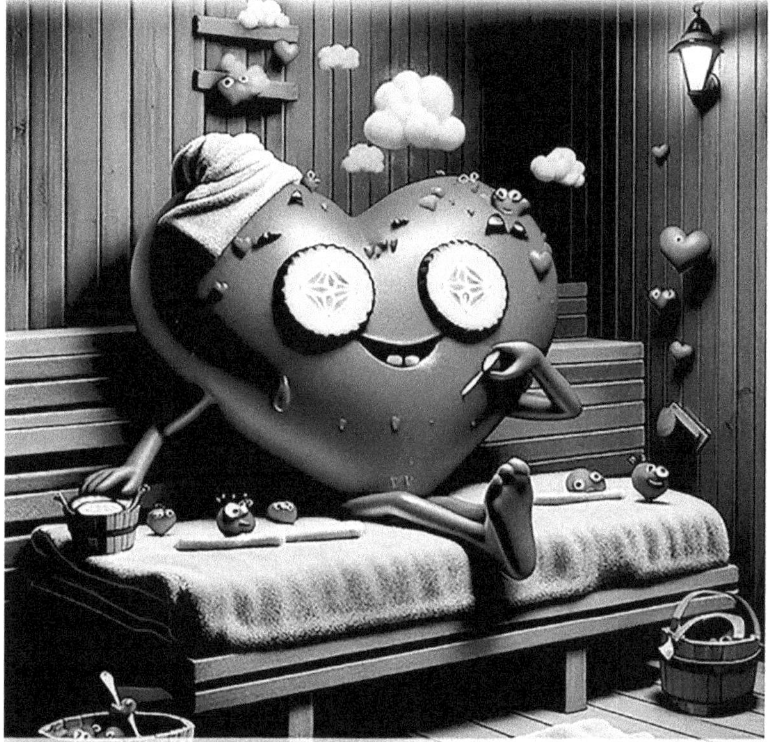

About David Strauss

When a falling rock collided with David's head while exploring ancient ruins, his 5-year recovery became his life's purpose.

DAVID...

An author coach, thought leader, and transformational speaker with a story of thrills, resilience, and transformation. David's life reads like an adventurous novel, filled with twists and turns that shaped him into the transformational author, coach, mentor, and Life Strategist he is today.

From Tragedy to Triumph

At just 15, David's world crumbled with the death of his mother. Facing life alone as a runaway at that young age, he summoned a relentless spirit that propelled him through high school, college at CU Boulder, and into a world of boundless exploration.

A Brush with Death, A Gift of Destiny

While exploring ancient ruins, a falling rock struck David's head. The rockfall was a defining moment that created the opportunity for David to reinvent himself, beginning with those daring moments at ground zero of his collision with the rock. This incredible journey has forged his philosophy as a thought leader.

Scaling Heights, Diving Depths

David's zeal for life extends to scaling the 23,000-foot summit of Aconcagua, Argentina, plunging into the depths with SCUBA, and taking leaps from planes and bridges through skydiving and bungee jumping. His adventurous pursuits are metaphors for his Life Coaching philosophy: Embrace life fearlessly.

Philanthropist and Community Volunteer

David's world travels and philanthropic endeavors reveal a man dedicated to elevating humanity through both personal growth and social impact. His extensive community service and global outreach are a testament to his commitment to making a difference.

- Tim Tebow Foundation

- Make-A-Wish Foundation

- CU Cancer Research Foundation

- National Multiple Sclerosis Society – Fundraising Athlete

- Boulder Youth Shelter - Pier Role Model Volunteer

- American Heart Association - Fundraising Athlete

- San Diego Homeless Shelter - Fundraising Athlete

- Boulder Meals-on-Wheels Volunteer

- Big Brother Volunteer

- Boulder Youth Shelter Volunteer

- YWAM – Youth Volunteer for disadvantaged kids in Wellington, New Zealand

- Colorado Educational Foundation – Fundraising

- Key-Note Graduation Speaker at Emily Griffith Center for Disadvantaged Youth in Larkspur, Colorado (2000)

- Previously sponsored by Pearl Izumi, Schwinn, EMS, United Airlines, Air New Zealand

Begin your journey with David's Coaching and Mentoring

CONNECT NOW!

DavidStrauss.com